Malik hadn't slept in three days. He hadn't eaten in two days. He hadn't killed in one day. But that was all about to change. *First the kill, then the meal, then the sleep,* Malik chanted to himself dogmatically. He glanced over at his partner, Livien. Her eyes were bloodshot and ringed in dark circles, but she seemed alert. Malik could tell that she was thinking the same thing as they crouched silently in the mud, stalking their prey.

The pair had been in the Ring for almost three weeks. No Human team had ever gotten so far in the Ring before. The stakes were high – if Malik and Livien were the last ones standing, humankind would be rewarded with the entire planet for colonization. Their victory would give humans a real home, the first one since abandoning a desolate and uninhabitable Earth hundreds of years ago.

The only things that stood between humanity and its dream were the last contestants left in the Ring. Over a hundred species had entered and now it was all down to Humans, Ursks, and Eirlons. Malik hadn't seen any trace of the Ursks since day four, but they were the least of his concerns right now. His eyes followed the Eirlon male through the sun-dappled swamp, waiting for the ideal moment to strike. The Eirlon moved slowly, as though searching for something. The female Eirlon was limping behind him, blood oozing from her left leg. She paused, dropping down on one knee. The male turned to help her. Malik saw his opportunity.

Silent and quick, Malik sprung from the foliage with his makeshift spear and stabbed the Eirlon male through the neck. As the Eirlon gurgled his last breath, Malik felt a pang of sympathy. Of all the alien races, Eirlons resembled Humans the most, at least on the outside. *But they're not humans*, Malik reminded himself as he turned to the female Eirlon. One glance told Malik she was already dead on her feet –

the wound on her leg was infected beyond salvation. A few more hours and she would be dead. It was a mercy when Malik thrust a bone dagger through her heart.

Malik turned, expecting to see Livien walk up behind him with a smile on her face. After all, they had just come one step closer to victory. But, Livien wasn't there. Adrenaline still pumping through his veins, Malik searched for her where they had been crouching moments before. She was gone. His heart leapt to his throat in panic – and then he saw her.

"LIVIEN!" Malik screamed, not caring who or what might hear him. He ran heedlessly through the swamp towards Livien's swinging body. She was strung up by her neck in a tree, her clothes all but torn off and her body twitching. The pale sheen of her skin was a beacon against the cold gray background of the swamp. Malik's training flew in the face of seeing Livien dead. Instead of thinking about who killed her, all Malik could think about was how he couldn't let her die.

Malik never made it to Livien's body. The Ursks's poisonous tusk gored him through the stomach as he ran straight into the trap. The look of surprise never left his face, even as he drifted towards death. *We were supposed to win,* Malik's last thoughts insisted. *We were supposed to live.*

*Chapter One*
*Present Day*

Acara flung her body to the side just as her attacker landed a heavy punch where she had been lying a split second ago. She had already taken a couple hard hits and she wasn't sure she could withstand one more. Acara always hated this portion of her training – unarmed combat was never her forte, given her petite size and short reach. Her size was even more of a disadvantage in this particular match against Axton, who stood at over six feet tall and was made entirely of tightly wound muscle.

"Come on, that's all you got?" Acara taunted a bit more breathlessly than she intended. Her right hand clenched instinctively and she could feel the force building in her fist, but she held back. It was against the rules to use biotic enhancements during unarmed combat, which was another thing Acara hated about these matches.

*Why be a Silver if you can't even use your abilities?* Acara complained silently, gritting her teeth.

She knew she looked tired and disheveled, with her long, jet hair falling out of her normally pristine bun and sweat dripping down her entire body. But this was the point in the fight when most opponents underestimated her, and she was counting on Axton to do the same.

"Price, you never give up, do you?" Axton smiled, using Acara's surname. He circled Acara cautiously. This wasn't the first time he had sparred with her and he knew she always had a trick up her sleeve. After all, they had been best friends since childhood. Axton still remembered when he was a kid and Acara used to beat him in every match. That was before his growth spurt. Acara had grown, too, over the years – her skinny frame had filled out in all the right places. It was those curves that were Acara's biggest advantage over Axton, although she didn't seem to know it.

"Are you going to stare at me all day or are you going to spar?" Acara teased.

Axton scowled. It was foolish to think that a girl as beautiful as Acara didn't know her effect on men. He charged. Acara stepped aside casually, having anticipated Axton's move. She used Axton's momentum against him and he landed flat on his face. When he raised his head, blood was coursing from his nose, but he didn't miss a beat. He lashed out with a fist, catching Acara on the tender part of her torso where he had already hit her before. A flash of pain crossed her face, but instead of giving in, Acara slammed her knee against the back of Axton's neck forcing him to eat floor once again.

"Attention all Candidates, please report to the main hall immediately for an important announcement. This is a Code Green. Repeat, report to the main hall immediately regarding a Code Green," a voice sounded in Acara and Axton's communication implants.

"Damn! I had you," Acara cursed. She helped Axton to his feet.

"Do you think it's legit?" Axton asked doubtfully. In Axton's twenty six years of life, there had been over a dozen Code Greens and each had been a false alarm.

A Code Green meant that the Intergalactic Council had found an inhabitable planet. Of the billions of planets in the universe, relatively few were inhabitable and even fewer were unoccupied by intelligent life. If this new planet was both inhabitable and unoccupied, it would mean that Axton and Acara would have the opportunity to compete in the Ring. The Ring was all they had been training for their entire lives. The Ring was destiny.

"Let's go find out!" Acara said, racing Axton to the main hall. All the other Candidates were streaming in the same direction, chatting excitedly about the Code Green.

Acara's heart fluttered as she passed under the doorway to the main hall, walking below a plaque with an emblem of Earth and the words "Semper Domum Redi" – "Always Return Home." Hundreds of years ago, after decades of wars and environmental abuse, Earth became too desolate to support life. The death toll in those years was astronomically high. Eventually, the remaining leaders of the world banded together with a plan to abandon Earth in search of a new planet. Humankind took to space in a fleet of Lightjumpers, the most advanced of Earth's spaceships, in the hope of finding a new home. It didn't take long before humanity figured out they weren't the only ones in the universe seeking refuge.

The Intergalactic Council picked up the Human ships not long after the Exodus, and humankind joined the ever-growing, ragtag space fleet of the Displaced. The Displaced Armada was made up of the remnants of hundreds of alien species who had lost their home planets for one reason or another. Each species was searching for a new home, and the Intergalactic Council created the Ring as a way for them to earn one. The Ring was a fair way for species to fight for a planet that minimized bloodshed and circumvented war. It also safeguarded the Council's interests and territories by keeping the Displaced from trying to colonize inhabited planets. After all, the members of the Council were all "landed" species, already possessing their own home planets.

The rules of the Ring were simple – once an eligible planet was discovered, the Council would launch a Ring to the planet, marking a perimeter in which the contest would take place. Each of the Displaced could send two representatives to the Ring, one male and one female. A battle to the death would ensue and the last species standing won the rights to colonize the planet. Participation in the Ring was strictly voluntary. While some species were fine with living on spaceships for the rest of their existence, most were able to find two representatives to compete in the Ring. Every once in a while, a species would strike out on its own in search of a new planet rather than play by the Intergalactic Council's rules. But, without the Intergalactic Council's support and supply chain, those species would inevitably fail and wither away in the depths of space.

For Acara, Axton, and the other Candidates, the Ring was a calling, something they trained for almost their entire lives. In the eight hundred years since the Exodus, Humans had participated in six Rings. The first Ring was a disaster – the Humans were completely unprepared for the evolutionary superiority of many of the alien species. After that first humiliating loss, the Human government set up the Candidate program as an offshoot of the military to train prospective Ring competitors. But by the fifth Ring loss, humanity rebelled against the idea of the Ring and sat out the next two rounds of the Ring, disbanding its Candidate program and preaching the virtues of living peacefully on ships. But the political pendulum swung back full force fifty years ago, and the Candidate program was reinstated with a renewed vigor. And now, after the sixth Ring and the near-victory of Malik and Livien, both national heroes, the Candidates were better than ever.

"Hey, watch it!" Acara griped as someone pushed past her. The guy turned around and sneered. Acara rolled her eyes. Deimos was notoriously nasty and Acara wasn't surprised that he'd pushed her, especially with their history. Deimos, one of the physically strongest Candidates in the program, had always been someone Acara would never like or trust. He rarely spoke but he managed to bully everyone regardless with the sheer brutishness of his demeanor.

"Want me to punch him in the face for you?" Axton gritted his teeth behind Acara. Acara turned and smiled, knowing that Axton had sparred with Deimos more than once and never emerged the victor.

"Save it for the Ring," Acara remarked.

Once all the Candidates were gathered, the President appeared on the projector walls of the circular hall, his face visible at every angle. The room became quiet instantly.

"Candidates, many of you are probably wondering if this Code Green is your call to destiny or a false alarm," the President began, drawing out the suspense. "The Intergalactic Council has indeed confirmed the discovery of a new planet XD-3011. The Council has also announced that, after several weeks of study and observation, XD-3011 has breathable air, potable water, and arable land. It is also devoid of intelligent life. The Ring has already been launched to the planet's surface and in two Earth weeks' time, two of you will be sent to represent humanity in the greatest challenge of our existence."

A second of silence as the words sank in was followed by the uproar of cheers and stomping of feet. Axton wrapped Acara in a giant bear hug, lifting her off her feet. It took several minutes before the celebrating calmed down enough for the President to continue.

"This Ring will be unlike any other because the stakes are higher than any other. XD-3011 is the largest inhabitable planet discovered in several thousand years, three times the size of our Earth. It is rich in natural resources and could sustain a population larger than we ever had on Earth. This is our opportunity to build a new home. Candidates, you have been training your entire lives for this moment. You are ready. The human race is ready. This is our time!"

A deafening roar of approval rose up from the crowd. The President's image faded from the projector walls, replaced by the Earth emblem. A circular podium lowered from the ceiling into the main hall. Standing tall on the podium was a stern, white-haired man. His weathered skin was pulled taught against his hard face, the face of a man that never smiled. The man didn't have to wait for the hall to quiet down – Candidates knew to snap to attention when the Commandant was present. He didn't clear his throat to speak, choosing instead to bark the first word out of his mouth.

"CANDIDATES!" the sound of the Commandant's gritty voice reverberated around the room. He paused for effect then continued. "The President thinks you're ready for the Ring. I don't. None of you are ready for the Ring. I don't think you're strong enough. I don't think you're fast enough. And I *know* you aren't smart enough. All these years, I've been training you and you've been a constant disappointment to me. I haven't seen a single Malik or Livien amongst you. But I can't control when the Ring happens, so you're all I've got.

So I guess that makes this your lucky day – you have a chance to prove me wrong!"

"Inspiring," Acara muttered sarcastically to Axton. Axton smirked until he saw the Commandant's eagle eye land on them. The Commandant continued his speech, but Axton knew the Commandant had made a mental note of them. Nothing ever escaped the Commandant's attention.

"Over the next week, you'll undergo grueling tests that will test your physical and psychological limits. You will be weeded out one by one until two of you prove to me that you are worthy of representing the human race. If I were you, I would rest up today because tomorrow may very well be the very worst day of your lives. Dismissed!"

The Commandant disappeared with the command podium, leaving the Candidates to speculate about what was in store for tomorrow. Few details ever slipped out about the pre-Ring test, or as the Candidates called it, the Gauntlet, and the ones that did got lost among the false rumors and gossip. But, most candidates knew enough about the Gauntlet to know that the Commandant wasn't exaggerating – tomorrow would indeed be a bad day.

Chapter 2

*Acara*

Later that night, Acara sat with Axton in the mess hall, sharing a meal of dehydrated steak and test tube grown potatoes. The room was abuzz with Candidates discussing tomorrow's Gauntlet and Acara found it hard not to think about it as well. She stared at her reflection in her metallic food tray as she chewed on the too salty steak. Bright caramel eyes framed by long swooping lashes stared back. Her golden complexion was clear except for a small mole on her cheek, a constant annoyance to Acara. She supposed she should be thankful, though, that her skin was unmarred by the scars that many other Candidates accrued in the years of their training. But she certainly didn't look like the "ultimate survivor." She looked like any other girl.

But she wasn't just any other girl. She was groomed to be a Candidate since before she was born. Most Candidates were picked up when they started showing precocious abilities in school, around six years old. Only a handful of people, commonly referred to as Silvers for the color of their biotic manifestations, were specifically bred to become Candidates.

Silvers were always a controversial topic for politicians within the Earth Fleet. Created from in utero exposure to dark space radiation, a process so dangerous that fetal death resulted in over 99% of cases, many people believed that Silvers were abominations. There was a clear divide in public opinion – for every person who denounced the creation of Silvers as humans "playing God," there was another who lauded it as the next step in human evolution. It wasn't really a topic anyone sat on the fence about.

Even within the Candidate program, there were as many staunch proponents as there were opponents, despite the fact that the program had the highest concentration of Silvers in the Fleet. The rift between Silvers and regular Candidates was noticeable even in the mess hall, with both groups tending to sit with their own cliques. Acara never quite understood why the dynamic between both groups was so mistrustful – the only real difference between a Silver and a regular was their degree of biotic ability. Even the most untalented regular Candidate could use biotic abilities given an amplifier. She supposed the naturally competitive nature of the Candidate program only served to exacerbate whatever small differences existed, though.

As one of the few Silvers born in her generation, Acara received special treatment from the second she first drew breath. Before she could talk, she was fitted with her first amplifier. Before she could walk, someone was teaching her the first of five alien languages. Before she could run, she was learning basic electronic engineering. Before she could fight, she knew how to kill a man in ten ways with only two fingers. Acara was born to go to the Ring.

Turning her attention away from her own reflection to Axton's chiseled profile, she couldn't help but feel that he was how a Ring Champion was supposed to look. Axton's build was a perfect inverted v shape, molded through years of hard training and discipline. His dark hair was slightly too long to be within regulation, but combined with his gray eyes, it gave him an air of rebellion that girls swooned over.

Axton was also a consummate womanizer, plowing through string after string of girlfriends since the age of thirteen. Acara liked to joke that hers was the longest relationship Axton had ever had with a woman. It would have been funny if it hadn't been so tragically true. Unlike Acara and the other Silvers who had been raised by the government since birth, Axton had had a mother growing up. Ever since his mother's death, Acara had been the only girl in his life. She had always been content being his best friend, but lately she had been noticing him in a new way – one that made her pulse beat a little quicker. It scared her and thrilled her all at once.

*I wonder if he ever thinks about me that way,* Acara asked herself. It was a question she would never have the courage to bring up to Axton in a million years.

The chatter in the mess hall became markedly quieter as a dark shadow seemed to enter the room. Acara looked toward the doorway where Candidates were parting to make way for someone ... Deimos. He stalked into the hall with latent animosity as though daring someone to get in his way. Of course, no one did. Everyone knew better.

Deimos was notorious throughout the Candidate program for his ruthlessness. He was indoctrinated to the program at the relatively late age of eleven, after he had been expelled from his third civilian school. No one knew what he had done to get himself noticed by the Commandant, but the rumor was that he had killed someone. Acara had no doubt that he was capable of it – at eighteen, he was one of the youngest Candidates, seven and a half feet of muscle and rage.

"I hate that guy," said Axton, glaring at Deimos as he walked menacingly forward. Axton's entire being pulsed with a silver aura, the pupils of his eyes taking on a metallic sheen. Most people wouldn't have noticed, but Acara could sense the biotic discharge right before it happened – Axton was never good at controlling his abilities in the heat of anger.

"He clearly feels the same way," Acara commented, noting the look Deimos returned in their direction. Deimos harbored a special hatred for Silvers, as they were the only Candidates that posed a threat to his supremacy. Not that any Silver, including Acara and Axton, ever defeated Deimos in an unarmed match. But allowed biotic amplification, they came dangerously close.

"Let's go," Acara urged. Tonight wasn't a good night for a confrontation, and judging by Axton's fidgeting, a confrontation was definitely on his mind.

With reluctance, Axton allowed Acara to guide him out of the mess hall, avoiding Deimos like the plague. Acara couldn't help noting with satisfaction all the disappointed and lustful eyes that followed Axton out of the room.

*Sorry, ladies,* she thought to herself, feeling as far from sorry as anyone could.

## Chapter 3
### Acara

Acara woke up at the crack of the artificial dawn blooming from her translucent cabin walls. She brushed her teeth and washed her face like it was any other day, but her heart was already racing in her chest. Today, she had a date with destiny.

"Hey, wake up, it's time to go!" Axton's voice sounded in her comm piece.

Acara hurriedly pulled on her uniform, a mottled gray jumpsuit with camel colored boots, and opened the door. Axton's smiling face greeted her on the other side.

"We still have an hour!" Acara complained as she pulled her hair into a bun.

"I knew you would already be up," Axton replied. "Let's go get breakfast."

"I don't know if that's a good idea – what if they make us spar first thing? I'd hate to spar on a full stomach."

"And what if this test lasts the entire day and you're not allowed to eat at all? Come on!" Axton grabbed Acara's hand and pulled her along. She hated that he was so much bigger than she was, his hand enveloping hers completely. She also hated that she kind of liked it.

As they walked together to the mess hall for breakfast, Acara wondered if Axton was as nervous as she was. He would never admit it, so there was no point in asking. Acara knew him too well – one of Axton's biggest strengths was his bravado. He embodied everything that a Silver should, especially the quality of supreme confidence.

As far as Acara was concerned, there were two ways to intimidate opponents, especially among other Candidates. You could be like Deimos and intimidate through fear with brute strength and cruelty. Or you could be like Axton, who intimidated through sheer force of personality and a casual certainty of victory. Axton's self-assurance stemmed from his unwavering belief in destiny, and that his destiny was to win the Ring. Acara envied that confidence – as much as she tried to convince herself of the idea of "destiny," she didn't really buy it.

"You look stressed out, Price," Axton told Acara over breakfast. She scowled, pushing her oatmeal around her bowl. "You shouldn't be. We're going to win the Gauntlet. And then the Ring."

"You're deluded," said Acara.

"I'm confident," answered Axton, so sincerely that Acara felt a little better. Acara looked into his eyes, a light steel color under the fluorescent lights. They seemed so certain. Acara sighed.

*No wonder why girls swoon over Axton,* Acara thought, *the man has never doubted himself in his life.*

Acara and Axton lapsed into silence as they hurriedly finished their breakfasts. Too soon, it was time to go.

After a short journey down the paneled hallways of the Earth mothership, the pair arrived at the Testing Station, a part of the vessel dedicated solely to the Gauntlet. No Candidate ever went in unless there was a Ring looming.

"Name?" asked a uniformed attendant at the door.

"Acara Price."

"I need to take your amp, Lieutenant Price," said the attendant, checking off her name on his holographic tablet.

Acara removed the metal bracer from her forearm and placed it in the attendant's outstretched hand. He looked at the holoscreen for verification of her identity, and then carefully placed it with the others in his bin. The other Candidates entering the Testing Station looked slightly uncomfortable surrendering their amps. While all Candidates had some amount of biotic talent, only Silvers could make use of biotics without the amplification device. Acara imagined the others felt quite naked without their amps.

Axton and Acara found their places within the ranks of Candidates standing in formation inside the Testing Station. Though the Candidates' excitement was palpable, the room was silent. No one really knew when the first test began.

The click-clack of steel-heeled boots signaled the arrival of the Commandant, accompanied by a dozen Trainers and two Intergalactic Council representatives. By law, the winning species of the last Ring were supposed to supervise the next Ring, making the Ursks the Council representatives on board. The two Ursks were greeted with hostile stares from the Candidates.

"Good morning, Candidates," the Commandant began.

"Good morning, sir!" all two thousand Candidates replied in unison.

"Our honored Intergalactic Council representatives would like to have a few words with you before we begin," announced the Commandant, with an emphasis on the word "honored" that implied the opposite of its meaning. It was no secret that the Commandant was close friends with Malik and Livien before they were killed in the last Ring by the Ursks.

If the Ursks noticed the disdain, they didn't seem to acknowledge it. The taller one stepped forward and addressed the Candidates.

"The first procedure in getting ready for the Ring is to disable your communications implants," said the Ursk. "Usually, this is only done for those going into the Ring, but your Commandant has asked that yours be disabled before your Gauntlet as part of your test. You will hear a small pop in your ears now, followed by some ringing. This is normal."

The Ursk pulled out a handheld device and quickly pushed a sequence of buttons.

"Agh!" Acara yelped, clutching the side of her head. It felt like a small explosion went off in her ear. She looked around to see all the other Candidates doing the same thing.

"Atlaak'l lo periut'tuh zo," the Ursk ended, satisfied. Most of the candidates looked confusedly at each other. Acara knew enough Ursk to know that he said, "It is done."

Without the communications implants to translate alien languages automatically into each Candidate's brain, many Candidates would not be able to communicate with alien species at all. They would also not be able to receive messages from Command or communicate with each other through the implants. This change was a double-edged sword for Acara. On the one hand, it gave her a significant advantage over other Candidates because she could speak several alien languages fluently. On the other, it put her and every other human at a disadvantage to those alien species who could communicate telepathically without an implant.

"For the slow learners in the room, our dear Ursk friend has just taken away your ability to understand alien-speak," continued the Commandant. He would have smirked at the Candidates that were still clutching their ears, if smirking was something that he did. "The Gauntlet begins ... now!"

As soon as the Commandant said "now," Acara could hear a metallic hum coming from the edges of the room. Suddenly, the air filled with the sound of hundreds of short hisses. Confusion broke out amongst the Candidates while the Commandant stood calmly on the command podium with his delegation.

The girl standing in front of Acara suddenly collapsed without a word. Acara bent down to help her, even as more Candidates began to fall. Acara flinched back as a blur whizzed by her face. It was a dart. It lodged itself in the thigh of the girl to her left and the girl went down instantaneously. Acara flattened herself against the floor just in time as another dart hummed over her head. Face pressed to the ground, Acara struggled to see what was happening around her.

Seconds later, the hisses stopped. The metallic hum ended soon after.

"Candidates! Atten-tion!" the Commandant barked. Acara stood up cautiously, even as some of her classmates sprang crisply to attention. More than half of the Candidates were still on the ground, unconscious. "Congratulations! Take a look around. If you're still standing, you've passed the first test. Some of you were quick thinkers. Some of you were ruthless. Some of you were lucky. You'll need all three qualities to win the Ring. Trainers, take command!"

As the Trainers called out names, Acara took the chance to glance over to the male formation. She breathed a sigh of relief as she recognized Axton in the crowd. Axton turned just in time to lock eyes with Acara and wink. Acara rolled her eyes.

"Axton Fontaine!"

Axton trotted over to a group of nine male candidates and followed a Trainer through to the next chamber.

Acara's name was called soon after. As she disappeared through a door with her group, she glanced behind her. Some of the Candidates on the floor were just now regaining consciousness. Acara watched as a girl sat up in confusion, her face crumpling into tears at the realization that she'd already been cut.

Quickly, Acara turned away from the scene and surreptitiously examined the girls walking beside her. Most of them she recognized from classes. Almost all of them were taller and more muscular than Acara, but she'd never lost to any of them in a sparring match before. Only one other girl was a Silver and she didn't look very intimidating with her pudgy roundness and ridiculous blue hair. Acara felt a little better.

"I don't belong here," the blue-haired Silver walking beside Acara whispered urgently, evidently noticing that Acara was sizing her up. Acara looked at her incredulously. No one ever said stuff like that as a Candidate, especially not a Silver. It was tantamount to saying you were a loser.

"I didn't even know what was going on. It's just that the girl in front of me fell on me and her body pinned me down on the ground," the girl continued. Acara was mortified. She didn't know how to respond, so she nodded silently in what she hoped came across as understanding.

"I'm Juna," said the girl, sticking out her hand. Acara looked at Juna's hand, then at the other girls walking around them clearly eavesdropping on the conversation. She looked back at Juna's face – there was something there, and it wasn't what Acara expected. Her meek smile was a little too practiced, and something in her oily eyes seemed too eager.

Acara hesitated. Juna's arm was still extended conspicuously. A hurt expression crossed Juna's face as she realized Acara wasn't going to shake her hand.

"Hi, I'm Linnara," the tall brunette behind Juna interjected. She had, of course, been listening to the whole exchange and her sympathy for Juna was etched in her frown lines. Juna turned around and offered her hand and a waxy smile. Linnara shook it. A surprised look flitted across her face.

"Oh!" squeaked Linnara, just before she fell to the ground unconscious. Everyone stopped in their tracks, turning to stare at Linnara's prone body. Everyone except Acara. Acara's eyes never left Juna. Juna noticed and waved, smiling even wider as Acara caught the gleam of the metallic dart Juna had palmed in her hand.

The Trainer doubled back to see what the commotion was.

"We need a medevac in the Testing Station, corridor B," the Trainer announced into her communications implant. The Trainer checked to make sure Linnara was still breathing. When it became apparent that Linnara was fine, the Trainer ushered everyone along.

"We have a tight schedule, let's continue."

Everyone filed behind the Trainer without a backwards glance. Acara made sure she was the last one, keeping Juna in her line of sight.

## Chapter 4
### *Acara*

It had been two days since the first surprising test of the Gauntlet, and Acara was slightly relieved that every subsequent test had been more conventional. She breezed through the gamut of IQ tests she was given, solved each puzzle she encountered, deciphered each code she was told to crack.

So far, with the exception of the first test, the Gauntlet had been a breeze, which was precisely why Acara was filled with such apprehension. There was no way things would remain this easy for long.

"Are you going to feel jealous when I'm in the Ring with Axton?" Juna asked in a fake, sugary tone. She sashayed toward Acara, her blue bob swishing.

Ever since Acara had avoided her trap, Juna had been trying to get under her skin, making snide comments every time Acara was within earshot. Acara knew this game – Juna was going to try to psych her out and wear her down. But, it wasn't going to work. Ignoring detractors was a skill Acara had perfected.

"If you don't start talking to me, I'm going to begin to think we aren't friends," Juna continued.

Acara eyed Juna warily as she got closer. There was no telling what kind of dirty trick Juna would try to pull, and when. It was actually kind of exhausting, now that Acara thought about it, having to keep one eye on Juna at all times.

"And if we aren't friends, then I can't have you at our wedding when Axton and I get married."

Acara had to suppress a guffaw in response to the ridiculousness of Juna's attempts at provocation. First of all, Juna was not exactly physically attractive. She was a heavy set girl who looked very out of place among the other Candidates. While everyone else was trim and athletic, this girl was downright overweight – a trait that had been effectively bred out of humans decades ago. To see a portly human civilian was rare in and of itself – a chubby Candidate was almost unheard of. Secondly, if Axton wasn't turned off by Juna's looks, he would certainly be repulsed by her acerbic personality.

*If she thinks this line of goading is going to make me rise to her bait, she is simply dumber than she looks.*

But while Acara wasn't the least bit perturbed by Juna's words, the mention of Axton made her heart beat faster. She hadn't seen him since the Gauntlet began and she wondered how he was faring. There was no doubt in her mind that he would excel at the tests if they were anything like the ones she had been given thus far. But still, she worried. After all, the Gauntlet was unpredictable, even if Axton was not.

## Chapter Five
### Axton

Axton felt like he had been treading water for hours. His arms were starting to ache and his legs were all but numb in the freezing cold water. He didn't know what to do next.

The Water Survival Test had been a relative cakewalk up to this point. It started with a simulated river, where Axton had to fight against the current to reach the end. Axton had always been a strong swimmer but even he struggled against the jagged rocks and sudden bends in the river. The river ended at the top of a platform ten meters above another pool. Axton could see by the variation in the water color below that there was only one small area that was safe to land in. Everywhere else was too shallow.

After Axton had made the leap, the pool floor dropped and more water poured in, forcing him to tread. It was like he was a fly in a giant half-full glass of water, encircled by high walls on all sides.

Earlier, when he was less tired, he had tried to climb the wall. There were some grooves in the wall, but the metallic surface made it impossible to get a grip when wet. After his fourth failed attempt, Axton decided he must have missed something and did a lap around the entire pool looking for another way out. He couldn't find one.

Now Axton was exhausted and freezing. He wasn't sure what to do next. Even if climbing the walls was possible, Axton wasn't sure he had enough arm strength left to attempt again. His body was starting to shut down because of the water temperature. He had to get out of there. There had to be another way.

*What would Acara do?* Axton asked himself. *Acara would take one look at the wall and know she simply physically wouldn't be able to climb it. She'd try to get around it. But I already searched the entire pool! You can't get around it!*

*Acara would have figured it out ages ago*, thought Axton as he racked his brain. Acara was the smartest person he knew. She wasn't just book smart either, she was perceptive and quick-witted. More often than not, that quick wit was used against Axton, but he didn't mind her teasing.

Suddenly, it dawned on Axton. He was thinking like a man who thought he should be strong enough to climb over the wall. He should have been thinking like one who knew that strength wasn't going to get him past the wall. *If every Candidate has to pass the Water Survival Test, then there must be a way to get past the wall. It must be possible.*

Axton had already tried going over the wall and around it. But there was something he hadn't tried yet – under. He took a deep breath and submerged himself completely, the shock of the freezing water washing over his head almost forcing the air from his lungs. With one hand touching the wall, Axton propelled himself downwards. The water seemed unfathomably deep for a spaceship to hold. Axton struggled to keep his eyes open in the stinging water. Finally, he reached the bottom of the pool, but not before he reached the bottom of the wall.

*The wall doesn't reach the bottom!* Axton rejoiced. He swam beneath the wall, kicking hard, propelling himself forward even faster with a surge of biotic energy. His lungs were on fire. The space beneath the wall seemed to close in on Axton, pressing down on his back as he struggled to reach the light at the end. Bubbles escaped from his mouth, but still he kept going. He was not going to drown down here.

Finally, there was no wall above him. Axton pushed off the bottom of the pool with all his remaining strength and shot to the surface of the water like a cork. He spluttered and gasped for air. He was in a shallow pool now, the metal wall to his back and a sandy beach in front of him. The air was hot and the water was comfortably warm. His Trainer sat on the beach in a lounge chair, sipping on a fruity cocktail.

Axton stumbled onto the beach from the pool, spitting up water and coughing. The water dripped from his sopping wet uniform as he peeled it off his goosebump-covered body. The Trainer looked unimpressed.

"Congratulations, Lieutenant Fontaine. You passed the Water Survival Test," the Trainer stated matter-of-factly. "Took you long enough."

Axton nodded numbly, savoring the warmth of the beach as his body shivered uncontrollably.

"Are you ready to advance to your next exam?" the Trainer asked, although Axton got the sense that it was more of a rhetorical question.

"Yes, sir," answered Axton, teeth still chattering.

"Then head that way and join the rest of your classmates in the elevator."

Axton saw the elevator in the wall at the end of the beach. The doors were wide open but no one was inside.

"Sir, there's no one else in the elevator," said Axton, nonplussed.

"That's right. You're the only one in your group who passed this test," the Trainer replied. "Now go."

## Chapter Six
### Acara

Acara had been looking forward to this for days. She had endured round after round of medical screening and psychological tests – now it was finally time to fight. Normally, Acara wouldn't be this excited about sparring, but the idea of finally getting the chance to kick Juna's ass made her blood rise in anticipation.

The sparring chamber in the Testing Station was essentially comprised of a dozen partitioned compartments forming a circle around an ovular central viewing room. Every wall was transparent, allowing spectators in the central chamber to see into each room and those sparring to see into the rooms adjacent to them.

Acara listened eagerly as the trainer announced the rules of the test – it was to be a timed round robin type tournament where each Candidate would rotate through each compartment to fight someone new. She smiled to herself when she heard the trainer add that use of biotics was allowed. Given that regulars didn't have their amps, Acara had a significant advantage going in.

Luminescent lettering began to scroll across each glass surface of the sparring rooms, announcing who would be fighting against whom. Acara's heart leapt as her wish came true – her first match would be against Juna. Examining her opponent, Acara was not impressed. But, she had learned over the past several days in the Gauntlet not to underestimate Juna. According to the tests, Juna's biotic energy levels were off the charts. Spitefully, Acara speculated that Juna's extra weight was where she stored all that extra biotic energy.

The glass door sealed seamlessly behind them as the girls made their way to the center of the sparring room. Acara stared Juna down as the countdown started. Juna's face sported a bland smile but her body language oozed hostility. A static-like biotic discharge surrounded her hammy fist as a blade of energy manifested from her knuckle. Acara was both impressed and annoyed – she knew how hard it was to generate a Material Surge, especially one that looked and probably felt like a sword. She also knew that if Juna had enough energy to burn showing off rather than fighting, it was probably going to be a rough bout.

Juna was the first to make a move as the starting buzzer sounded. She darted forward, blade first, catching Acara across the shoulder and drawing first blood. Wincing, Acara berated herself for expecting Juna to be slower because of her appearance – biotics didn't discriminate against size. With a swift series of jabs, Acara retaliated.

The fight wore on, surprisingly even-matched given how different their fighting styles were. While Juna went on the offensive with powerful biotically enhanced punches, Acara retreated, reserving her energy.

"Tired yet?" Juna taunted, nipping forward with a spryness that belied her stature.

"Tired of seeing your face," retorted Acara, aware that it was a pretty useless thing to say. She jumped back, avoiding Juna's assault.

Minutes passed and both girls were breathing hard. Whereas Juna's strategy seemed to be to wear Acara down, Acara's strategy was to wear Juna out, making for an exhausting, if boring, fight. Besides the first hit Juna had landed, there had been no contact in the match.

Suddenly, Acara saw an opening as Juna's Material Surge began to flicker. Moving in quickly, Acara summoned biotic energy to her fist, catching Juna with a painful jab to the rib cage. She followed with an onslaught of hooks and punches, none of which landed as Juna manifested an energy shield around her body. Undeterred, Acara continued to attack until at last, one of her powerful uppercuts broke through Juna's defense and connected right beneath her jaw. Spittle flew from Juna's mouth as her head snapped back and she collapsed to the ground like a fallen tree.

"Match concluded. Winner, Acara Price," announced a disembodied voice over a loudspeaker.

Trying to be sportsmanlike, Acara stood over Juna and offered her hand. As soon as Juna clasped it, Acara realized that she had made a mistake, but it was too late. With leg sweep, Juna knocked Acara to the ground. Acara fell hard, banging the back of her head against the wall. With a feral scream, Juna launched herself on top of Acara, scratching at her with a Material Surge manifesting in long, bladed fingernails.

The sparring room was suddenly filled with a loud grating siren that made both Juna and Acara clutch at their ears in pain. Two trainers entered the room, apparently unperturbed by the cacophonous din, and separated the two girls.

"The match is over," a trainer reprimanded Juna. She stalked out of the room, but not without shooting a devilish grin in Acara's direction first.

Seething, Acara smoothed her disheveled hair as a medical engineer appeared. Using a metal wand, he scanned her body for injuries, stopping to inject Fillers into the cut on her shoulder and the bloody bump on the back of her head. Although the Fillers soothed her pain instantaneously, she hated the idea that millions of tiny nanobots were under her skin repairing her cells. The thought made her skin crawl.

Armed with the satisfaction that she had won the match, Acara forced herself to ignore Juna's underhanded attack and focus on her next opponent. As the desire to seriously harm Juna began to subside, Acara couldn't help but feel sorry for whoever showed up to fight her next. She had an awful lot of pent up aggression now, and she needed a punching bag.

## Chapter Seven
## The Commandant

"How many are left?"

"Only 84, sir."

The Commandant rubbed his chin. *84. That's less than I expected,* he thought. *But it's still 82 more than we need, I suppose.*

At 57 years old, the Commandant was every bit as intimidating as he had been in his youth. He still stood ramrod straight and moved with the same deadly elegance as a lion on the hunt. His hair hadn't thinned at all since his twenties, but it had become white as powder. When the last Ring had happened, the Commandant was a young man nearing his peak. He had passed every grueling test in the Gauntlet, but it hadn't been enough. Now, as he watched this new generation of Candidates, he wondered if any of them had what it took to win the Ring.

"Any promising Candidates?" the Commandant asked his Chief Trainer. Of course, he had already singled out the promising ones in his mind.

"Sir, there's quite a bit of talent in this pool. Candidate 22 has passed every test with flying colors – then again, it's to be expected as she's a Silver. She has excelled at the survival challenges and mental acuity tests. She speaks five alien languages fluently, and is proficient in at least eight others that we tested."

"What about her sparring matches? Hand to hand combat?"

"She tends to shy away from direct contact with the opponent. Candidate 22 has extremely fast reflexes and extraordinary control over her biotic abilities. She's one of the few Silvers that can create a Material Surge with her enhancements. But, in direct unarmed combat, she tends to falter – after all, she is limited by her stature. There is another girl in the same group, Candidate 31. She's a better offensive fighter than Candidate 22. She doesn't have the same intelligence, but she does have cunning. She took out another girl in her group before they even reached the first Gauntlet chamber."

"Really? Interesting. What did she use?"

"One of our darts."

The Commandant would have laughed if he hadn't quit the practice of laughter years ago. He sat pensively. The Chief Trainer's evaluation matched the Commandant's to a tee.

"Any others?" the Commandant demanded.

"Candidate 84 and 26 are also at the top. These women are more well-rounded than the previous two Candidates I mentioned, but they aren't Silvers. But, they *are* consistent. They are older, so psychologically and emotionally, they may be more prepared for something like the Ring."

"What about the male Candidates?"

"There are a handful of standouts. Candidate 3 is dangerous. He is physically the strongest out of the bunch and also the fastest. His reflexes are unreal – it's like he knows what his opponent is going to do before they do. And I haven't seen him get tired yet – not during a test, not during a sparring match, not during anything. He is a juggernaut. And to top it all off, he's not even a Silver. According to our monitors, he's only slept an average of three hours a night this entire time. But, according to our psychological evaluations, Candidate 3 is probably a sociopath or worse."

"Worse?"

"He shows psychopathic tendencies as well."

"Very interesting. Continue."

"Another standout is Candidate 72. He is almost as strong and almost as fast as Candidate 3 and he is completely emotionally stable. He doesn't have the ruthless cunning that Candidates 3 and 31 have, nor the intelligence of Candidate 22, but he has heart."

"Heart!" the Commandant spat out disdainfully.

"Sir, with all due respect, heart – or determination, resilience, persistence, whatever you want to call it – is as important as brains. Many Candidates didn't even get far enough to fail – they just gave up. Candidate 72 spent almost an hour treading water in the Water Survival course until he found a way past the wall."

"That's impossible. No one can withstand that kind of water temperature for an hour."

"Well, he did. I'm just saying that Candidate 72 is someone for whom failure is not an option. And I mean that in the most literal sense."

The Commandant harrumphed.

"Then there's Candidate 44," the Chief Tester continued. "He's smart. He's more than smart, he's a genius. He fashioned a laser gun out of scrap metal and spare electronic parts in less than twenty minutes. He can speak over a hundred alien languages fluently. Candidate 44 is a master of precision in combat – he can cut off the flow of blood to any extremity with a simple jab in the right place. He has won every match so far with less than three contacts per match."

"You mean he took down each opponent in less than three strikes?"

"That's correct."

"Is he a Silver?"

"No."

"That's ... actually quite impressive," the Commandant admitted.

"But he's a glass cannon. He can deal a lot of damage to an opponent through his pressure point technique, but he can't take a hit at all. The one time an opponent managed to land a hit on Candidate 44, he almost keeled over. He probably would have lost if he hadn't managed to cinch his opponent's artery earlier in the fight."

"Is that it?"

"Yes, sir."

"Promising."

"Yes, sir."

"You're dismissed, Chief."

The Chief Trainer bowed out of the command room, leaving the Commandant alone with his thoughts. The Commandant pulled up each Candidate's file on his command screen, going over them in excruciating detail until the faces and vital stats started to blend into one another. He was looking for something, some quality that he couldn't quite put his finger on. *These files don't tell me anything!* he thought in frustration. There was only so much he could learn about the Candidates by how far they could run or how hard they could throw a punch or how quickly they could solve a puzzle. He needed to know something more ... human.

There was one day left of the Gauntlet. There would be a final test like no Candidate in the Gauntlet had ever seen before. It was the last chance for the Commandant to find out what he needed to know before the Ring. And he would find out, no matter what the cost.

## Chapter Eight
### Acara

The past few days had been the most grueling of Acara's life. On top of the gamut of tests and sparring matches, Acara had hardly gotten any sleep because of Juna. Juna, who had taken out Linnara with an underhanded trick on the first day of the Guantlet. Juna, who had taken out two other girls since that day. Juna, who seemed to revel in accomplishing every challenge in the least honorable, most devious way possible. Acara was sick to death of Juna.

But, today was the final day of the Gauntlet and Acara was glad she would only need to deal with that little monster for a little while longer. There was only one test left and Acara was about to find out what it was.

"Acara, you look so ... tired," Juna sneered as their group, now whittled down to four girls, filed down the hallway. "Been getting enough sleep lately? Or too busy checking me out?"

Acara walked on, careful to keep a good distance between herself and Juna. Her silence did nothing to stifle Juna's verbal jabs.

"Not in the mood for chit chat? That's ok. You'll be rid of me soon enough. When I'm in the Ring and you're sitting in your comfortable space pod watching the entire thing over the holotube."

Refusing to be goaded into a response, Acara looked straight ahead and marched on.

"Hope you're ready for this last test – I heard they make you face your worst fear. What's your worst fear, Acara? I bet I know what it is. It's me, isn't it? Remember that time I almost killed you in the sparring room? You should have seen your face."

"I will always beat you," snapped Acara. She rounded on Juna, but still kept her spacing. "I will always beat you because you're predictable. I would just think of how a coward would fight and then I'd know your next move. And then I'd destroy you."

Juna laughed in response, snapping her fingers in mock applause.

"She speaks! Finally! After almost a week – I'd almost given up on you. You know, I think that ..."

But Acara didn't have to listen to what Juna thought – they'd finally arrived in the main hall and the sight of the other remaining Candidates shocked even Juna into silence. There were less than fifty Candidates in the room and everyone looked like hell. Bruises, cuts, and scrapes adorned almost every face that turned to see the last group to enter the hall. No one was talking and everyone looked around nervously as though suspecting a trap. After all, this gathering could be a prelude to the final test or the final test itself.

There was only one face that Acara wanted to see, only one face that mattered. It didn't take long for her to find it – Axton's dimpled smile was a beacon in the otherwise sullen crowd. Acara grinned. She wanted to run into his arms but instead she approached cautiously.

Acara couldn't remember the last time they'd been apart this long. Since their first meeting, the two had been inseparable. Every birthday, every holiday, every significant event in their adult lives had been experienced together. Even when Axton went on dates, he'd call Acara for her advice or, more likely, an excuse to end the date. It felt strange now, having gone through possibly the biggest milestone in her life, for Acara talk to Axton. She wanted to tell him everything, but really, it was weird that he didn't already know everything.

"You look like crap," Axton teased, embracing Acara gingerly instead of with his usual bear hug. Acara could tell it was because Axton was covered in bruises under his uniform. He had the beginnings of a black eye from one of his sparring matches and the beginnings of a beard from a week of not shaving. Even then, Axton was more handsome than any man had a right to be after the worst week of his life.

"There's no way I look as bad as you," retorted Acara, though she instantly felt self-conscious. She hadn't seen her reflection since the Gauntlet started, but she could only imagine the bird's nest of her hair and the dark circles under her eyes.

"How many Candidates are left in your group?"

"We have four left. You?"

"I'm the only one – have been since the water survival test," Axton said with some pride.

"Well, watch out for that one," Acara warned, tilting her chin in Juna's direction. "She's a real piece of work."

"Thanks for the heads up. I ... I'm really happy to see you," admitted Axton somewhat awkwardly. Acara was still close enough to him that she had to tilt her head up to make eye contact. She lowered her gaze as soon as she heard his tone soften, uncomfortable all of a sudden with the emotion in his voice.

"Not that there was ever any doubt!" Acara joked nervously.

An awkward silence followed. It was soon interrupted by the tell-tale click-clack of the Commandant's boots hitting the floor. All the Candidates turned to face the front of the room at the same time as though a silent order had been given. The Commandant surveyed the group in front of him, his expression inscrutable.

"This gauntlet started with two thousand Candidates and you handful are all that are left. You should feel proud to have made it this far. You have faced real challenges and real danger. However, it has not been enough. You have one last test, only one more obstacle in your way, and you must now make a choice. This test is completely voluntary. You don't have to do this. No one will think you a coward for opting out. Some of you have families to consider. Some of you can make a more significant contribution to humanity than going into the Ring. All of you have bright futures ahead of you."

Acara shot a look at Axton. *What is he talking about?* she tried to communicate through her eyes. Axton shrugged.

"No Candidate has ever faced this test before – you will be the first. None of you have killed before. This test will give you that opportunity. Which means that some, even many, of you will certainly die during this test."

Acara raised her eyebrows. No matter how hard or dangerous the Gauntlets were, no Candidate had ever died during one before. The med techs made sure of that.

"So now you make your choice. Follow me to the last test, or stay here, go back to your lives, your families, your futures. If you choose to stay, you will be given your assignment of choice with the Human Fleet and an honorable commendation for your efforts here in the Gauntlet. It is your choice to make and whatever you choose is neither right nor wrong, honorable nor dishonorable."

With that proclamation, the solid wall behind the Commandant parted and he and the Trainers curtly turned heel and walked through it down a long hallway. There was a moment's hesitation amongst the Candidates before someone made the first step to follow. It was Deimos. His face betrayed no emotion but his step belied his excitement. Acara felt Axton take her hand for a brief moment and squeeze it. She didn't have to look at his face to know it was set with determination.

As Axton stepped forward, Acara looked around to see who else would do the same before she followed him down the hall. Every few paces, Acara would look back to see who else was behind them. As expected, she glimpsed some familiar faces like Juna and the other girl in her group whose name she never caught. But the line was thin – it was clear that not every Candidate was willing to walk to their potential deaths just to risk their lives again in the Ring.

The group finally stopped as the long hallway intersected with a perpendicular corridor with doors along one side as far as the eye could see. Each door was numbered, but not in numerical order. The Trainers directed each Candidate to a door. Acara was sent to door 22, which happened to be between door 72 and 31. She gave Axton a look that she hoped communicated all the things she was feeling and was rewarded with another of his brilliant smiles. *If anyone is going to get through this, it has to be Axton,* Acara thought to herself. *He's not afraid of anything.*

Acara scowled when she saw that Juna was at the door right next to hers – 31. She allowed herself one moment to exchange dirty looks with Juna before she focused on the door in front of her.

After all the Candidates were situated outside their respective doors, the Trainers left. Acara looked down the corridor – only about thirty Candidates lined the hall. She could have sworn more than that had followed her from the main hall, but she couldn't be bothered to think about it. She was too nervous.

The doors in front of the Candidates opened with a gush of stale air. Acara peered inside hers and could see nothing but pitch black, even with the light of the corridor behind her.

"Step forward through your door," the unmistakable voice of the Commandant boomed over the loudspeaker.

Acara breathed out shakily before she stepped forward. Immediately, the door behind her snapped closed and she was plunged into total darkness. Tentatively, Acara reached out in front of her and met a wall. She stretched her arms to the sides and almost immediately hit the wall on either side. The space around her was a box no bigger than the door she had entered through. Claustrophobia had never been one of Acara's concerns, but the tight space coupled with the complete darkness would have been disorienting to anyone.

The box started to move, lurching forward, then upward, then left, then right, until Acara was no longer sure where she was in relation to her starting point. Acara leaned against the wall, feeling slightly motion-sick, until the box stopped moving as abruptly as it started. The wall Acara was leaning against suddenly disappeared. Tumbling forward, Acara found herself in a small room filled with blinding white light and mirrored walls. As her eyes adjusted to the sudden brightness, she could see that the room was completely empty except for an unremarkable podium against the far wall.

"Step up to the podium," the Commandant's voice reverberated around the chamber.

The top of the podium slid open and something arose from its depths, something that had been outlawed for centuries.

"A ... gun?" Acara said aloud, disbelieving. She had read about guns in her history classes growing up – on Earth, people had used them to kill each other. Countless millions of deaths were caused by gun violence over Earth's bloody history. So many people had died during the Last World War that guns were made universally illegal. No guns were brought on the Exodus ... at least, that's what Acara was taught.

Acara removed the gun from the podium. She handled it carefully, more like a bomb than a gun, as though it might explode in her hands. It was heavier than it looked and ice cold to the touch. She fingered the trigger lightly. *This is the difference between life and death,* Acara wondered.

"What you now have in your hands is a gun. This artifact is dangerous. It ended millions of lives on Earth and contributed to the downfall of humanity. As you know, guns are banned from modern society. But in the Gauntlet, those rules don't apply. Here is your final test: on the opposite side of the wall in front of you is your opponent, your target. You have one bullet in your gun. Kill your opponent. No matter who or what appears in front of you, shoot it. That is all."

It seemed like a simple enough task, but the way the Commandant emphasized "no matter who or what appears" bothered Acara. She chewed her lip, thinking. *Obviously, whatever lies in wait on the other side of the wall is supposed to be a challenge to shoot. Not a*

36

*technical challenge as guns won't be allowed in the Ring anyway, but maybe an emotional challenge?*

"The wall in front of you will disappear in five seconds. Good luck," the Commandant ended.

A woman's voice started counting down.

"5 ... 4 ..."

*Whatever I see on the other side is supposed to shock and surprise me. I'm not supposed to want to kill it. Or him, or her, or whatever.*

"3 ... 2 ..."

Acara screwed her eyes shut and held up the gun in shooting position. It was a gamble. But if she was supposed to find it hard to shoot what she saw, maybe it would be better if she didn't see at all.

"1!"

Acara pulled the trigger, her eyes still tightly closed. The gunshot echoed. Her eyes snapped open and she froze in shock, the gun falling from her hands. She was looking at Axton who was looking back at her, stunned. A burgundy stain was slowly spreading from the center of his chest. It was blood.

"AXTON!" screamed Acara, as the moment unfroze. She ran to him just as he collapsed on the ground. Cradling his head in her lap, Acara tried to staunch the bleeding from his wound but it pooled around them at an alarming rate. She screamed for help, for a medic, for the Commandant, not even noticing that all the walls in the room had become transparent and all the other Candidates were now visible down a long hallway. Each pair of Candidates had an identical setup to the one Acara was in.

"Please don't die, Axton, please," Acara cried, nuzzling her face against his. He was pale, a thin sheen of sweat coating his face. Every breath seemed to pain him more than the last. Acara wasn't even sure he knew she was there.

After what seemed like hours but could only have been a minute, a medical team rushed in and took Axton away. Traumatized, Acara could do nothing but stare dimly as they wheeled him out of the room. Slowly, she became aware of dozens of eyes on her. The other Candidates peered through their transparent walls, trying to get a glimpse of the commotion. Acara stood, her hands still dripping Axton's blood. She looked around numbly.

In all the rooms she could see, there were two Candidates standing. There was no blood, no medics rushing in and out. No one else had fired the gun as far as she could tell. Acara's eyes locked on Juna's in the compartment next to hers. Juna looked back, an astonished look on her face. Juna's counterpart, a willowy teenage girl, goggled at Acara in revulsion. Acara felt her heart drop. No one had fired, not even Juna.

Acara was the only murderer.

*Chapter Nine*
*The Commandant*

In the 34 years since the last Ring, the Commandant's life had been a study of the contest. He spent countless hours every day watching and rewatching footage from past Rings, hoping to discern some nugget of wisdom that would clinch the win for humankind. He didn't just examine the human teams, either – he knew the ins and outs of each species' capabilities and strategies. *If I were twenty years younger, I would be the best Candidate for this Ring*, the Commandant thought wistfully. But he'd already had his chance and he knew it.

As much as it pained the Commandant to do it, the last test in the Gauntlet was a cruel necessity. He needed to find out who could kill. If there was one thing he learned from watching the footage from past Rings, it was that humanity was weak. The people who were picked for the Ring were heroes. They embodied love and loyalty and selflessness and teamwork, all the great "human" qualities that citizens strived for. When heroes killed, it was because of a greater cause, but it wasn't in their DNA. Killing never came naturally to heroes.

*If Malik hadn't put Livien's life ahead of his own, we might have won the last Ring*, the Commandant thought to himself bitterly. The Ring was a game of survival above all else. Anyone not looking out for his own survival was bound to lose.

"Chief, I've come to a decision," the Commandant announced, leaning back in his chair.

"I know, sir," the Chief Tester replied.

"Wipe that look off your face, Chief. You know as well as I do that the last test told us more about the Candidates than all the others combined."

"Yes, sir."

39

"Then stop looking at me like I'm some monster."

"Yes, sir."

The Commandant sighed. Of course the Chief had some differing views on a test where the Candidates shoot each other with illegal weapons. *It's not like I forced them to do it,* the Commandant thought irritably. *And in the end, only two of them pulled the trigger.*

"Sir, I must insist you reconsider. I know the Candidates you have chosen," pleaded the Chief Tester. "But they are not of the same ilk. Candidate 22 had her eyes closed when she pulled the trigger – had she seen who was on the other side of the wall, I have no doubt she would not have fired. She's not a natural born killer. Candidate 3 is. He's not just a killer, he's a cold-blooded killer. He *likes* to kill. And not only that, I have reason to believe he would be indiscriminate in his killing as well. Partnering them in the Ring would be dangerous for the girl."

"Being in the Ring is dangerous for anyone, Chief. Besides, the girl pulled the trigger, that's enough proof for me. She can obviously take care of herself; we've seen that from her performance in the Gauntlet. And if she can't, well, we only need one of them to survive the Ring. And I believe strongly that Candidate 3 is humanity's best hope for victory. You said it yourself, Chief – he can't be stopped."

"Nor can he be controlled, sir."

"That's enough, Chief. I've made up my mind," the Commandant snapped. The Chief swallowed his disagreement and bowed silently before leaving the room. The Commandant rubbed his forehead in frustration. He had expected the Chief of all people to understand. Someone had to make the tough decisions.

The Commandant picked up the framed photo of himself, Malik, and Livien on his desk. It was the only piece of memorabilia he allowed himself. He traced their faces with his leathery finger. Malik and Livien's deaths would mean something now. So would the deaths of all the other Ring contestants in the past, now that someone had finally learned the hard lesson that their deaths taught. Heroes wouldn't win the Ring. But killers would.

## Chapter Ten
### Acara

The past week was by far the worst of Acara's life. Thousands of times worse than the week of the Gauntlet. Ever since the Commandant had announced her as his choice for the Ring a week ago, her life had been turned upside down. Some Candidates congratulated her, but most kept their distance. Between the people whispering behind her back and the ones openly worshiping the ground she walked on, Acara had never felt so lonely or so ostracized.

It hadn't taken long for word to spread of what she did to Axton in the Gauntlet. Her only consolation was that everyone treated her Ring counterpart Deimos even more coldly. She couldn't blame them – the rumor was that Deimos had shot his opponent point blank in the face, killing him instantly. Axton, thank goodness, was still alive, albeit in critical condition.

Acara couldn't think of Axton without feeling sick to her stomach. She would never have pulled the trigger if she had seen him on the other side of the wall. Afraid to face him, Acara secretly visited Axton's hospital room every day but never let him see her. She didn't know how he would react – after all, she was the person who ended his lifelong dream of going into the Ring. She was supposed to be his best friend ... and she shot him. Nothing she did from here on out would ever change that cold, hard fact.

The last thing Acara wanted to do was to attend the Ring Banquet tonight. But it was her duty as a champion of the Ring. The Ring Banquet was the most lavish event humanity put on, one that occurred only once or twice in a lifetime. Everyone who was anyone would be in attendance. It would start with a feast of epic proportions and end with the Ring champions leaving for the Council Mothership in their final journey before the Ring. The whole night would honor the two Ring champions but Acara couldn't imagine herself getting any enjoyment out of it. Not without Axton.

Acara put on her ceremonial uniform and examined herself in the mirror. Even she was impressed with how "champion-like" she looked. The crimson robe hung off her shoulders and plunged into a deep v at her chest. The silky material wrapped around her waist and emphasized her curves in the most flattering way, while the floor length of the robe masked her high heels, making her seem taller and more regal. Intricate embroidery flowed through the robe, telling the story of past Ring champions in a beautiful web of shining threads. She looked strong yet feminine, exactly how she had envisioned herself as champion.

What she couldn't envision, however, was Deimos as the other Ring champion. For her part, Acara had gone out of her way to try to discuss a strategy for the Ring with Deimos after they were announced as Ring champions. It only took one interaction before Acara realized that Deimos was not someone that could be a partner. Something was off about Deimos – he exuded a cold, dispassionate hostility that made him impossible to trust. In fact, something about his empty black eyes actually scared Acara. There was only one word she could think of to describe Deimos – soulless.

*How different this would have been if the other Ring champion had been Axton*, thought Acara wistfully.

"It's time," a nasal voice sounded from the other side of Acara's door. Ever since her communicator had been disabled, Acara had to be assigned a handler to make sure she was on schedule. Acara's particular handler was an overzealous ginger girl with a horribly grating voice.

"I'm coming," answered Acara, hoping her response would be enough to keep her handler from talking more. With one last look in the mirror, Acara left her room for quite possibly the last time ever. There would be no returning after the banquet – she would be ferried straight to the Intergalactic Council mothership, and from there, into the Ring itself.

After a short shuttle ride, Acara and her handler reached the Grand Atrium of Earth's mothership. Acara had never seen it look so splendid. Row after row of banquet tables were laden with food and adorned with colorful centerpieces made of exotic live flowers that were specially cultivated in the ship's greenhouse. The ceiling was covered in tiny lights, flickering in merry imitation of the stars outside the ship. Instead of their everyday drab uniforms, the people seated in the hall wore colorful finery, some of which had been original cultural clothing passed down for generations. From brightly patterned kimonos to shiny taffeta ballgowns to dashing tuxedoes, every guest was clearly dressed to impress and for good reason – there were cameras and reporters everywhere snapping shots and broadcasting live to households throughout the entire Earth fleet.

As Acara descended the stairs into the Atrium, she could hear the excited voices below reach a fever pitch as the guests noticed her arrival. Acara's handler guided her to a long table situated perpendicular to all the others at the front of the Atrium. Acara could barely suppress a grimace as she saw Deimos approaching the table from the opposite staircase, guided by a handler who was clearly terrified of him. It was no wonder – even in the flamboyant champion's robe, Deimos looked murderous. The two champions were seated side by side at the center of the table, the closest they had been to one another since the Gauntlet began. Acara mumbled a "hello" just to be polite, but wasn't surprised when she was met with no response.

"Ladies and gentlemen, humans throughout the fleet, I give you our Ring champions – Acara Price and Deimos Godson!" the emcee's voice boomed. The crowd erupted in applause and cheering as Acara and Deimos stood dutifully and waved, fake smiles pasted on both their faces for different reasons.

Acara zoned out as the emcee began talking about Acara and Deimos's lives and accomplishments. She scanned the room and recognized some faces in the crowd – the seats closest to the head table were filled with important political and business leaders, high-ranking military officials, and great thinkers and luminaries of the time. One table was reserved especially for the Candidates who had gone through the Gauntlet, with the ones who made it furthest at the head of the table. Acara knew she would find who she was looking for there – Axton. He still looked weak and shaky, seated in a wheelchair and attended by a nurse. Acara couldn't help feeling annoyed at the nurse every time she would touch Axton, even if it was to adjust his IV drip. While every other guest in the room was staring at Acara and Deimos in admiration and curiosity, Axton kept his eyes on the plate in front him.

"And now, the ceremony will begin with the traditional Bearing of the Gifts. Each representative of the four Ring virtues will present their offering to our revered champions and bless them with the traits that they represent."

At the emcee's cue, four officials entered the room in ceremonial white robes, each embroidered on the back with a different colored ring. The first stepped up the table where Acara and Deimos stood.

"I am the President of the Earth fleet, and I represent hope. My gift to our champions is a light that will guide them through dark times," the President said somberly as he presented two scrolls to the champions. Acara knew it was a contract that ensured when she returned from the Ring, all her needs would be provided for until death. If she didn't return, the same benefits would go to whichever beneficiary she chose to appoint.

"I am the Head History Keeper of the Earth fleet, and I represent knowledge. My gift to our champions is immortality in the hearts and minds of our people," the second official spoke. An image projected on the walls of the Atrium of Earth's past Ring champions. With a flick of his wrist, the Head History Keeper made Acara and Deimos's faces appear on the wall after Malik and Livien's. The crowd cheered.

"I am the Provisionary of the Earth fleet, and I represent perseverance. My gift to our champions is a taste of victory," said the third official. He motioned to a line of waiters who brought forth plate after plate of food that Acara had only ever seen in history books before. Delicacies like lobster and caviar were followed by fresh fruits like pomegranate and caramelized bananas and all sorts of foods that were not only rare but mouthwatering.

*This might be the only good part about becoming Ring champion,* Acara thought to herself.

The last official to present his gift was the Commandant himself.

"I am the Commandant of the Earth fleet, and I represent strength. My gift to our champions is the mark of their legacy," the Commandant thundered, louder than all the officials before him. He grasped Acara's hand first, turning her arm over to expose the underside of her wrist. With one deft motion, the Commandant pressed the face of the ring he wore on his left hand to Acara's wrist. She sucked in her breath sharply as she felt the ring sear her skin, and when the Commandant removed his hand, she saw the emblem of the Earth fleet burned into her flesh in a raised silver tattoo. After the Commandant performed the same ritual to Deimos, he raised both of their arms in the air to show the crowd.

"TO LIEUTENANT PRICE!" the Commandant roared. The crowd repeated his words, their applause a deafening rumble rolling through the Grand Atrium.

"TO ENSIGN GODSON!"

The crowd got louder.

"TO VICTORY!"

The crowd's cheers turned into gasps of surprise and delight as holographic fireworks lit the air above their heads and images from pre-apocalyptic Earth flashed around the room. Servers in white uniforms filed down the banquet hall tables bearing even more succulent food. The party had officially begun.

*I might as well eat if I have to sit here,* Acara thought to herself as guest after guest presented themselves to the head table to wish the Ring champions luck for tomorrow. Even though she was preoccupied with thoughts of Axton and playing nice for the civilians, Acara couldn't help but enjoy the sumptuous meal in front of her. It was the first time she had ever tasted real lobster or enjoyed the vintage of rare Earth wine she sipped on. She tasted a little of everything that passed before her – raw oysters that the waiter told her tasted like the "ocean," whatever that meant, seared kobe steak that melted in her mouth like butter, juicy pears drizzled in real honey. Such delicacies were specially cultivated on one of the agricultural ships in the fleet and just a mouthful would normally cost more money than a Fleet lieutenant could expect to make in a year.

Hours later, the banquet guests started to get rowdier, having gorged themselves on food and alcohol. The line to speak to the champions finally thinned as people started to hit the dance floor. At last, Acara had the opportunity to do what she'd wanted to all night – talk to Axton. He was still sitting at his seat, picking at the crème brulee in front of him, refusing to make eye contact with Acara. Well, she would make him look at her now. It was her last chance before the Ring and she couldn't lose it.

"Hi," Acara approached tentatively as she knelt beside Axton.

Silence.

"I'm sorry," said Acara, trying again. "I know how much you wanted to go to the Ring and I took that away from you. I'm really, truly sorry, Axton. "

Axton sighed and finally turned to meet Acara's gaze. She was shocked at what she saw written on his face. She had expected anger, fury, or hate, but there was nothing in Axton's expression but a deep, heart-wrenching sadness.

"The Ring!" Axton spat in disgust. "You think this is about the Ring, Acara? You shot me! You almost killed me!"

"I didn't know it was you – I had my eyes closed!" Acara tried to protest in her own defense.

"Oh, an accident. Right. Is that why you never bothered to visit me in the hospital? Did you even care if I pulled through?" asked Axton, his tone anguished.

"I ... I'm sorry. I did care. I *do* care," Acara amended lamely. Axton looked even more crestfallen, as though Acara had just disappointed him.

"No, you don't, Acara. You never cared for me like ... like I wanted you to. I can't do this anymore."

"What does that mean? You're my best friend, Axton!"

"Was. I was your best friend. Goodbye, Acara," Axton replied, turning away. Acara reached out and grabbed Axton's hand, clinging desperately as though he might disappear if she let go. Her heart was pounding in her throat and tears stung her eyes. She could see the tenseness in Axton's neck as he looked away from her, as though it was a physical effort from him not to turn back.

"Please, Mr. Fontaine is still in fragile condition. I'm going to ask you to step away now," Axton's nurse gently pried Acara away. Still shell-shocked, Acara didn't even have the presence of mind to object. She just stared numbly as the nurse wheeled Axton's chair away from her.

"Axton!" she cried, but her voice was drowned out by the crowd of revelers around them. People whirled and danced all around her, but she was suddenly more alone than she'd ever been in her life.

## Chapter Eleven
### Acara

Acara awoke, feeling the kind of refreshed one only feels after a drug-induced slumber. When she blinked the sleep away from her eyes, she found herself peering through a glass panel at a completely foreign environment. The events of last night rushed back to her as she gained her bearing – Axton abandoning her, the Ring officials sending her off in a shuttle pod, seeing the Intergalactic Council mothership through the pod window even as she was put to sleep.

The inside of the Council's mothership looked nothing like Earth's. Whereas Earth's ships were all smooth, plated surfaces on the inside, the Council's ship looked fleshy and organic. The hallways were round tunnels with wall surfaces that looked wet and gleaming. The only source of light came from glowing veins running along the walls, pulsating almost imperceptibly.

With a slight hiss, the door of Acara's shuttle pod opened and Acara took her first step onto the mothership. The ground felt solid and dry despite its sweaty sheen. To her left, Deimos was exiting his egg-shaped pod looking as inscrutable as ever. All around them, Ring champions from dozens of alien nations were emerging from shuttle pods. Even though there must have been over a hundred of them, Acara could name most of their species and associated strengths and weaknesses. Her eyes lingered on a pair of aliens whose species eluded her – they must have joined the Displaced after the last Ring because she didn't recall ever seeing them before. They stood almost fifteen feet tall, dwarfing the next largest Ring competitors. While their build seemed humanoid in stature, their entire bodies were covered in hardened plates. Their faces, if they had them, were hidden under layers of exoskeleton which made their heads appear disproportionately large. Acara made a mental note to find out who and what they were as soon as she could.

A sound like a wet belch signaled the arrival of the Council representatives as they popped out of the walls in front of the Ring competitors like bullets piercing through gelatin. There was one Council representative for each species. The one in front of Acara was a skinny, winged creature with orange skin and a mop of blue hair running from its head down to its tail.

"Greetings, Human champions," the creature uttered in perfect English. "I am your Ring representative. My job is to help you prepare for the Ring and make sure you are in compliance with all Ring regulations. Please, follow me."

The representative walked back through the wall, gesturing with its tail at Acara and Deimos to follow. Acara walked through the pulsing barrier, expecting an unpleasant sticky feeling but instead felt warm and dry, as though she had passed through a cotton ball. When she reached the other side, she followed the representative to a pair of clear tubes each large enough to fit a person inside.

"The purpose of the scanning tube is to ensure that no contestants enter the Ring with unauthorized items. Please step inside," the creature offered.

Acara stepped toward a tube, unsure of how to enter. The representative motioned Acara forward with a wave of its tail. Acara placed her hand on the tube and it sucked her in like the wall had. The tube started to fill with a blue gel and as it covered her mouth and then her nostrils, Acara panicked. Through her gel-muffled ears, Acara heard the representative say something about breathing normally. To her surprise, breathing through the gel was no different than breathing regular air.

Acara could see Deimos suspended in the other tube and her eyes widened in shock. His clothes were rapidly dissolving in the gel. Acara looked away, embarrassed, only to realize that her clothes had all but disappeared. She moved to cover herself but her arms and legs were stuck in position.

"Stay calm. I am simply removing all non-organic items from your person. I understand that humans have a nudity issue, so Council-approved clothing will be provided for you," said the representative. Acara wasn't sure what a smirk looked like on that alien face, but she was pretty sure she saw one.

A tingling sensation enveloped Acara's body as the "Council-approved" clothing weaved itself around her skin. Threads of black and white joined together, criss-crossing to make a steel gray jump suit that covered the skin from Acara's neck down to the tips of her toes. From what Acara could see of Deimos's suit, the outfit left little to the imagination. As the process finished, the blue gel started to drain and Acara could feel herself being excreted from the tube.

"You may remove your clothing at will by peeling away the seams along the waist or shoulders. It will offer you no warmth and no physical protection. Its sole purpose is to be a shield for your … dignity," said the representative. Acara was sure now that the expression it wore was indeed a smirk.

The representative held up two packs. Each pack had two compartments with small nozzles at the top of each compartment. The compartments were mounted on a bag roughly the size of a human school backpack made of slick waterproof material.

"Each Ring contestant receives a survival pack. The sack is empty and for your discretionary use. It is waterproof, fireproof, bladeproof, bulletproof, and basically indestructible. The compartments on the outside contain two Earth liters of water in one and liquid food in the other. These compartments will dissolve when empty. The pack will mold to your body when activated. To remove it, simply peel it away."

Acara stood still as the representative held the bag up to her back. Soundlessly, the bag attached to Acara's back as though suctioned on. It felt almost weightless and shifted with Acara's muscles, blending in seamlessly with her movements.

"You are now Ring-compliant. Follow me back to the shuttle docking station," the representative ended matter-of-factly, disappearing once again through the wall.

Back at the docking station, the representative continued as soon as Acara and Deimos emerged. Acara let her mind wander as the representative launched into a history of the Ring. She scoped out the competition, scanning the docking station tier by tier. While there were many fearsome looking species, there were also some downright cute species. Acara gawked at a pair of Mosqurats who were no bigger than children, with saucer-like eyes that were the only facial features that could be seen through their coating of baby blue fur. Most of the aliens looked humanoid, albeit with scales and tails and other genetic accoutrements. To Acara's surprise, most of the other species chose to wear the "Council-approved clothing." Even the Dondarian species, of which it was impossible to tell the males and females apart, were covered in dark gray.

Acara did a double take as her eyes landed on a pair of competitors that looked human. *Those must be the Eirlons,* Acara deduced. Eirlons were supposed to be almost identical in genetic makeup as humans, according to the books. The Eirlon male had a wave of dark hair and bright violet eyes that Acara could see even two tiers away. He stood a little more than six feet tall and had a muscular but trim build. By Earth standards, he would have been considered very handsome, but Acara guessed by Eirlon standards, he was a runt. The female standing next to him was a good head taller and several inches thicker around the waist, biceps, and thighs.

Suddenly, the male locked eyes with Acara. She stared back with curiosity, unable to look away from his mesmerizing purple gaze.

"This is important, so listen up," the representative snapped as it noticed it had lost its audience. Acara glanced over at Deimos and saw that he too was scanning the competition, but with a look of hunger rather than curiosity in his eyes. "There are three things you need to know about the Ring. One, the Ring will get smaller every day, forcing the competitors to confront each other. Two, everything in the Ring is indigenous to the planet. The environment inside the Ring remains untouched by the Intergalactic Council. Some of the flora and fauna may be harmful to your health. And three, at random times throughout the competition, the Intergalactic Council will broadcast a list of the species still in the game via sky hologram. The only way you can win the Ring is if every other species is eliminated. Any questions?"

Acara shook her head while Deimos merely glared.

"Then good luck," nodded the representative, motioning toward the shuttle pods. Deimos stepped inside his immediately, but Acara hesitated. She chanced another look at the Eirlons but they had already entered their pods. Acara could swear she saw a glint of violet as she turned away.

*Get your head in the game*, Acara silently berated herself. She let the pod enclose her inside, relaxing her body as she felt the gravity disappear inside the shuttle. The pod sank into the floor slowly until Acara was enclosed in darkness. She could feel herself sink further and further, until suddenly the pod shot into empty space with a pop.

Acara could see other shuttle pods speeding alongside hers as they hurtled together past a myriad of alien ships toward the huge planet in the distance. The planet was like all the photos she'd ever seen of Earth in its prime, with white clouds swirling above a blue and green backdrop. It looked larger than life. It looked like home.

## Chapter Twelve
### Acara

It was more beautiful than she could have ever imagined. As Acara's pod floated gently down from the heavens, she could see the turquoise water below and the silvery blue forest stretching out for miles in front of her. Every so often, crystal spires of the lightest purple punctured the forest canopy, rising like the ancient skyscrapers on Earth. The boundaries of the Ring were pulsing an electric blue in the distance. Acara estimated that the distance from one side of the Ring to the other would be at least sixty miles, a massive circle that encompassed both land and sea. The center of the Ring seemed to be directly below Acara, the point at which the beach melted into the water.

As her pod descended closer to the planet's surface, Acara noticed quartz-like blocks at the water's edge. Only a few jutted out of the water, but they were arranged such that they resembled giant steps leading into the shallows. More blocks could be seen strewn about the beach, half hidden by the black sand. Darting among the blocks were hundreds of translucent bubbles that Acara knew contained alien technology that would broadcast the Ring live to the Displaced. The bubbles would become invisible as they attached to each contestant, following them until the end.

With a soft thud, Acara's shuttle pod landed on the sandy shore and opened on contact. Acara blinked at the sudden brightness of her surroundings as she took her first step onto land. The soft sand was hot against her skin. She took a second to dig her toes in and feel the cooler sand below as she evaluated her surroundings. Deimos stepped out of his pod a few yards away from Acara. A few empty pods were already sitting in the shallows, but it seemed she and Deimos were still among the first pairs to land on the planet. Shuttle pods dotted the sky, still drifting gently from above. Most of them looked like they would land near the beach.

"We need to get off this beach and find cover before the others land," Acara took charge. Deimos glowered at her and then did something very strange – he smiled. Actually, it was more like he bared his teeth in her direction. Acara felt immediately as though something was terribly amiss.

"Actually, Acara, I'm going to need your pack," Deimos growled threateningly.

"What are you talking about?" said Acara, backing away from Deimos instinctively.

"Do you know why I signed up for this?" asked Deimos, his smile becoming more twisted as he spoke. "Because I like to hurt things. I like to cause pain. I like to kill. And here, I can kill everyone and everything with no consequences. Hell, they'll think I'm a hero for it back at the Fleet. So you can give me your pack and run, or I'll kill you right here and take it from you."

Acara looked at Deimos in horror. She always knew something was psychologically wrong with him, but she never thought he would be this murderous. She had to think, fast.

"But what about the Ring? What about winning?" Acara asked, stalling for time. She knew she couldn't outrun Deimos. But maybe she could outsmart him.

"Luckily, winning goes hand in hand with killing in this game. And only one of us needs to be alive at the end. Guess which one of us it will be?"

"If I give you my pack, you will let me go?"

"Pinky swear," Deimos laughed venomously.

"Stay right there. I'm going to take it off and throw it at you," Acara bargained. Deimos stopped in his tracks, staring greedily at her. He, too, knew he was fast enough to catch her even if she ran with a head start.

Acara slowly reached behind her shoulder as though to remove her bag.

"I don't have all day!" Deimos barked.

"I do," replied Acara calmly. She turned and bolted for the tree line, sprinting as fast as she could, her speed boosted by a biotic surge. Deimos made to follow but didn't get two feet before a shuttle pod fell directly between him and Acara. Another thudded to a landing behind him, and more were on their way. Deimos roared in anger and turned as the nearest shuttle pod's doors opened, revealing a slightly disoriented alien. It took less than two seconds for Deimos to snap the alien's neck, earning his first kill in the Ring. He ripped off the alien's pack and turned to ambush the next pod.

Acara didn't look back to see if Deimos was in pursuit as she crashed through the forest. The ground was a spongy consistency slippery with morning dew, making it hard to run, but she kept going. Leaves and branches whipped past her face, getting denser the further she ran, until eventually she couldn't see far enough ahead of her to keep up her pace. But before she could skid to a stop, she tripped on something solid and fell flat on her face into the muddy ground. Acara caught her breath. She had stumbled over a body.

The carcass was very fresh, which meant whomever killed it was still nearby. Acara turned over the body for examination. It was a Sarlek, one of the few non-humanoid species of the Displaced. It was shaped like a massive ball of flesh with millions of thin string-like cilia dotting its surface, allowing it to roll itself in its desired direction. In death, the Sarlek corpse had deflated to about a quarter of its normal size, yellow goo oozing out of a hole in its side. The deflated ball had three mouths, one gummy mouth meant for suctioning liquids and two mouths lined with serrated fangs the length of kitchen knives. The fangs were exactly what Acara needed.

Quickly and without hesitation, Acara forced a biotic surge to her right hand, making her fist harder than rock. She proceeded to knock the four large incisors out of the Sarlek's dead mouths. They were razor sharp. She gathered the stringy cilia from the body to use as rope, fastening three incisors to short sturdy sticks and one to a long straight branch. In just a few minutes, she had three makeshift daggers and a spear. The daggers went straight into her pack since she had no scabbard to place them in, but the spear was ready to use. Acara felt infinitely better now that she had a weapon or four.

Proceeding cautiously, Acara followed the signs of the scuffle deeper into the jungle. Judging by the tracks and the damage to the surroundings, quite a struggle had taken place not long ago. A few feet further, Acara found a sharp stick covered in yellow Sarlek blood. As she kept going, a sound caught her attention. It was a sort of sucking sound interposed with several loud cracking noises. Acara debated heading the other way, but curiosity got the best of her.

Pushing aside some palm fronds, Acara confronted a scene of carnage. There were three bodies collapsed in bloody heaps on the ground. Two were scaled lizard-like aliens with sharp beaks and even sharper claws. The third body was humanoid, but Acara could barely see it for the enormous fleshy boulder on top of it. That was where the sound was coming from – the remaining Sarlek was consuming the body of the dead alien, sucking blood and crunching bones with its three mouths. Acara fought a sudden wave of nausea as she stared in fascination.

A sudden flash of purple caught her eye. In the tree above the bodies, a pair of violet eyes stared at her. *Eirlons,* thought Acara, immediately scanning the scene for a second pair of those creepy eyes. She didn't need to look far – as the Sarlek shifted its weight on its meal, it revealed the corpse's white hair and female features. The Eirlon female.

Acara's gaze shifted back to the one in the tree and she took a closer look. The Eirlon had three ragged cuts across his shoulder and bicep, another deep wound across his chest, and a gouge dangerously close to his eye. Each breath he took seemed labored. When she listened, she could hear the thin branch the Eirlon was perched on creaking with strain. Scattered below the tree were the branches that had already broken under the Eirlon's weight. He would fall sooner or later, and it didn't look like he had the strength to win against the massive Sarlek if he did.

"Help me," the Eirlon mouthed to Acara. She shouldn't have been surprised that he spoke English – many alien species learned other languages. But he looked so human that she was caught off guard.

Hefting her spear, Acara charged out of the bushes and gutted the Sarlek. She sank the spear so deep into its body that there was only a half a foot left of the shaft sticking out. The Sarlek started to roll around, writhing in apparent agony. Acara was careful not to let it come near her with any of its mouths. She knew it was dead when it started to deflate like the corpse she had stumbled upon earlier. Her spear was sunk too deep to retrieve, and anyway, she didn't feel like cleaning it of the Sarlek's sticky blood, so she pulled a dagger from her bag.

*My first kill,* Acara barely had time to register before turning on her attention on the Eirlon. There would be time for contemplation later – more urgent issues were at hand.

"You speak English?" asked Acara. The Eirlon nodded, wincing with the movement. "Good. Then you'll understand this – I didn't kill the Sarlek to help you. I killed it because this was an opportune moment to eliminate it. Luckily for you, I'm not going to stand here all day and make myself a target for the others, so I'll be on my way. But if you come down here, I will kill you, too. Understood?"

"Where is your partner?" the Eirlon asked, seeming to ignore Acara's warning.

Acara started to walk away, stopping only to pick up the supply packs that the two lizard aliens still had attached to their backs. The female Eirlon's pack was ruined beyond repair and it seemed the dead Sarlek's pack had already been depleted.

"Stop! I can help you," said the Eirlon. "We can help each other."

"I don't need your help," Acara scowled without looking back.

She whirled as the sound of rustling leaves followed by a thud warned her that the Eirlon had jumped out of the tree. He was lucky the Sarlek's dead body broke part of his fall, but he still clutched his leg in pain. Acara stalked toward the Eirlon, shaking her head at his foolishness.

"Look at me. You know I'm not a threat," the Eirlon said, raising his hands above his head in a sign of submission. "You could kill me now, but I have a better deal for you. I can tell you where everyone is in the Ring."

"How could you possibly do that?" asked Acara doubtfully, despite herself. "And what makes you think I would trust you?"

"I have superior sight. I can see great distances, sometimes through solid objects ..."

"All that amazing sight didn't help you see the predicament I found you in, so what good is it?" scoffed Acara, interrupting the Eirlon.

"I can see ultraviolet light. For instance, I can see the camera bubble floating above your right shoulder," the Eirlon said, not missing a beat. Acara looked but saw nothing. "To anyone without UV vision, the bubbles are invisible. To me, those bubbles are like big glowing signs. And because I can see through several layers of this thick surrounding foliage, I can tell you that there are six other competitors heading in our direction, so we should start moving soon. As to why you should trust me – I'm badly injured. I probably won't make it far without your help, so it's in my best interest to keep you around. And I owe you my life, which is a debt I won't soon forget."

Acara lowered her dagger, chewing her bottom lip thoughtfully. If the Eirlon could be trusted, Acara could evade danger until the end of the Ring. She would be able to sit back and let everyone else eliminate each other. Best case scenario, she and the Eirlon would be the last ones left and she could take him easily. Worst case, she would be uninjured and well-rested going into the final showdown. It was a risk she was willing to take.

"You have a deal. But I still don't trust you. And let me make it clear – I won't hesitate to kill you if you cross me."

"Ka'el'Baleyden, but you can call me Kael," supplied the Eirlon, unbidden.

"Acara."

The sounds of approaching aliens were now audible. Acara helped Kael to his feet. His wounds were still bleeding. There wasn't time to do anything about the lacerations except slap mud over them and hope Kael wouldn't leave a blood trail. The two contestants quickly disappeared into the forest, Kael leaning on Acara for support.

They went on wordlessly for what seemed like hours, but could only have been two or three. The sky turned from a light pink to a dark maroon and finally a deep blue as the sun set and the twin moons arose. Kael was moving slower and slower and Acara couldn't support all his weight, even with her biotically enhanced stamina.

Eventually, the pair came across a half-dried up stream. Gnarled trees lined the banks of the stream, their twisted roots reaching for what was left of the water. Acara wriggled under the thick and mangled roots of an ancient tree to find that they formed a rather spacious cave underneath. She hissed at Kael to join her.

"We'll take cover here until it's light again," whispered Acara as Kael struggled to get in through the same small opening Acara used. "Here, you should eat something and have some water. You look terrible."

Kael looked surprised as Acara handed him one of the packs she had scavenged off the dead aliens. Grateful, he took it. Acara watched him for a moment as he ate in the light of his gently glowing purple eyes.

"Do your eyes always glow in the dark?" asked Acara after a few more seconds. She knew the answer, of course, but she wanted to test him a little.

"Yes," replied Kael. "I can control how bright they become, but this is as dim as they ever get."

Acara nodded. An honest answer.

"We need to do something about those wounds. I don't want them to get infected," Acara ventured after Kael was finished eating.

Kael looked at her again with that surprised expression.

"You're moving slowly enough as it is. If we keep up this pace, someone will catch us even if we can see them from a mile away," Acara explained, letting Kael know that she was just being pragmatic. "The mud seems to have stopped the bleeding but we can't just let those cuts fester. They need to be washed and bandaged. Here, take off your shirt."

Kael obeyed in silence. Acara couldn't help but admire his body as he revealed his defined torso and toned arms. It reminded her suddenly of Axton and a pang of guilt and regret made her go cold. She busied herself with cutting Kael's shirt into strips of fabric, separating the salvageable material from the ruined. Then she started to tend to Kael's shoulder wound. Dark red blood mixed with dried mud formed a crust around the three lacerations. With the clean water from the pack, Acara began to cleanse the wound. As the cuts were revealed, Acara breathed a sigh of relief that they were not as bad as they first appeared.

The chest wound was next and the injury was clearly more grievous than the shoulder wound. Blood oozed from beneath the mud covering, the cut was deep, and the edges around it were red and inflamed. Tenderly, Acara cleaned the wound but as she washed away the mud, the blood ran more freely.

"I'm going to look for the pressure point to cut off the blood flow to that artery and hopefully the bleeding will stop," Acara said as she began prodding Kael around the chest. Several minutes later, she seemed to have found what she was looking for. In one deft movement, Acara dug her fingers into two points on Kael's chest and he suddenly couldn't feel the pain in his chest any more.

"There, that should have worked. Guess we'll see if you bled out in the morning," joked Acara macabrely. She wrapped a makeshift bandage around Kael's broad chest, leaning in uncomfortably close to him to get the bandage around his back. When she looked up, she noticed Kael staring intently at her.

"What?" asked Acara.

Kael shook his head. With a shrug, Acara moved on to the cut above Kael's eye, wiping the grime from his face gently.

"Thank you," said Kael seriously, his eyes never breaking contact with Acara's.

The moment lasted longer than it should have and Acara broke away, unsure of how to respond.

"I'll take first watch," she said after a few awkward seconds, turning away from Kael. A few minutes later, Acara realized the cave had become suddenly darker. She looked at Kael – his bright eyes were closed in sleep already.

*How did this happen?* Acara asked herself. *Axton isn't here, my partner tried to kill me, and now my only ally is my biggest threat. This is all wrong.* The darkness she felt threatened to consume her as she wrestled with her predicament.

Kael snorted softly in his sleep, just once, but it was enough to bring an unsolicited half smile to Acara's face. It was at that moment

62

that she realized something unexpected – as much as she didn't want to trust Kael, she was glad she wasn't alone on her first night in the Ring.

## Chapter Thirteen
### Kael

The first rays of the morning sun started to stream in through the cracks between the tree roots, shedding light on the sleeping girl. Kael examined her for a while as she slept peacefully, noting in wonder how extraordinarily Eirlon she looked. Of course, Eirlon females were much larger on average than the human girl – Kael was still amazed that someone of her size could ram a spear almost all the way through a Sarlek.

Kael knew he was lucky the girl had come along yesterday when he was ambushed. His partner Seilke hadn't been as lucky. They had seen the two Sarleks' camera bubbles from a distance. While he had wanted to go around them, Seilke was adamant that they should confront them. She was convinced that their teeth would make good weapons or something. So they went after the Sarleks. It was easy enough to take one down with a sharp stick, but before Seilke could harvest the teeth, two more aliens appeared out of nowhere. With no weapons and no means of defense, Kael and Sielke were at a great disadvantage to the new arrivals and their razor sharp claws. It came down to throttling the aliens with their bare hands and both Kael and Sielke were severely injured in the process. If the second Sarlek hadn't joined in the fight, they both might have gotten away. But, the Sarlek did show up, and it and rolled straight over Sielke as she wrestled with one of the scaled aliens. Sielke was dead before Kael could save her. He could barely save himself, resorting to hiding in a tree to stay out of the Sarlek's reach.

While a part of him mourned the loss of his partner, the other part couldn't help blaming her for getting them into the dire situation in the first place. The Eirlon strategy had always been to avoid confrontation until the end. How else would Eirlons have consistently been among the last competitors in every Ring? Kael knew that going against that strategy would end badly, and Sielke proved it. He was just lucky he was still alive and now it was time to play the game his way, the Eirlon way.

The wound on Kael's chest throbbed. It wasn't bleeding anymore thanks to the human girl, Acara, but whatever she had done to it last night was wearing off. Kael looked down at his ankle and it was swollen purple and blue. It was probably sprained, maybe worse. That was not good. They needed to get to the crystal spire as quickly as possible and having an injured leg wouldn't help.

The cave was getting brighter now with the rising sun and Kael sensed it might be time to go. He took a quick look around to make sure there were no enemies nearby. The coast was clear. It was almost a shame to have to wake the human up – she looked so serene in her sleep.

"Acara," Kael whispered, touching her shoulder lightly. His pale fingers looked almost ghostly next to her warm caramel skin.

Acara's long lashes fluttered open and she looked confused for a moment to see Kael. Her hand tightened around her dagger for a brief second before her face registered some sort of recognition.

"Is everything okay?" yawned Acara, her voice still edged with sleep.

"Yes. But we must move quickly today," Kael said.

"Why, what are we running from?" asked Acara, suddenly alert.

"Running towards, not from. Did you see the crystal spire near the western edge of the Ring as we landed? The one that sticks out above the forest canopy?"

"Yes. What about it?"

"It's the highest point in the Ring. The only place where I will be able to get a full three-sixty degree view of the arena. From there, I can pinpoint where all the other competitors are. But we must hurry –

the Ring shrinks every day and I don't know how long it will take before the spire becomes out of bounds."

"That sounds ... like a decent plan," Acara agreed reluctantly. "What are we waiting for?"

"Nothing," said Kael, surprised at how easily Acara was convinced. "Let's go."

The sky was once again a pale rose color when the pair made their way outside. The sun streamed down through the leaves above, dappling the ground with dancing light. Kael was taken aback by how magnificent it all was, and when he glanced at Acara's face, he knew she was thinking the same thing.

"This way," Kael pointed. He started limping off, but Acara grabbed his arm.

"Wait," she commanded. "Stay here."

Kael watched Acara disappear in the opposite direction into the trees. He waited, confused, for what felt like a very long time but was probably only a few minutes. A twinge of doubt seized him as he wondered if she might have abandoned him. He could still see her camera bubble bobbing through the trees, though, which meant he could probably catch up with her if he followed her immediately. Kael was about to move when Acara suddenly reappeared, holding a wooden staff. It was about Kael's height, the silver bark peeled off to reveal a sturdy but supple core of indigo.

"This will help you walk," Acara said, handing Kael the staff. "Now we can go."

Acara walked off in the direction Kael had pointed to earlier, leaving Kael to stare after her in surprise for the third time since he met her. Kael knew that everything Acara did to help him was to help herself, too, but he couldn't help but wonder if she would have helped him regardless. The brusque way she tried to talk to him seemed too forced, as though her first instinct was to be kind to him.

66

Hours passed without incident as Kael and Acara trekked through the jungle, only stopping for Acara to lay traps for anything following in their wake. They made a solid team, with Acara cutting fluidly through the woods dagger first and Kael following behind on the lookout for danger. He only saw two camera spheres during their journey but they were far enough away that they weren't a concern. Kael hoped the whole trip to the crystal spire would be this easy, especially since once they finally arrived, he was pretty sure Acara would try to kill him. If there was one thing he knew about humans, it was that they didn't like getting lied to.

## Chapter Fourteen
### Acara

On the third morning, the first holographic Ring update was broadcast across the sky as Kael and Acara hiked their way through the jungle. They scrambled to a clearing between the trees to get a view of the transmission. Scenes of grisly demises played out across the horizon, final battles and last moments recorded across the Ring. Acara was not surprised to see Deimos's image appear in the sky as he killed over and over again, but she gasped when her own face appeared, contorted in effort as she speared the Sarlek. It seemed like forever ago. She had almost forgotten she had already killed someone and it shamed her to realize how little she cared. The next scene was of Kael's partner, the white-haired Eirlon, getting eaten alive by the other Sarlek. Acara silently thanked the Intergalactic Council for not broadcasting a soundtrack to go with the gruesome video. She glanced surreptitiously at Kael to see his reaction but his face was a blank.

The highlight reel of death was soon replaced by a hundred or more pictures dotting the heavens, representing all the Ring competitors. One by one, all the dead competitors began to disappear from the catalogue of faces. Almost a quarter of faces disappeared by the end, a good start by Ring standards. The one face that Acara was hoping to see blotted out still leered at her, though, a ghostly visage in the sky haunting her steps. She knew it wouldn't be so easy to get rid of Deimos, but a small part of her had hoped anyway.

The broadcast ended as abruptly as it began and the sky returned to its familiar and soothing pink. Acara and Kael returned to their hike.

"Your partner is still out there," Kael stated as though waiting for an explanation. Acara shrugged.

"Are you going to tell me what happened to him?" Kael probed further.

"Nothing happened to him," Acara replied curtly. She couldn't help but add, "Are you going to tell me what happened to yours?"

"Ah. Well, bad luck and over confidence would be the answer to that. Sometimes, the Eirlons chosen for the Ring are not the best equipped to survive in such a situation," said Kael cryptically. Acara could tell he was baiting her into a conversation by being vague. She managed to hold her tongue for ten seconds before giving into her curiosity.

"How did you get chosen for the Ring?" Acara finally asked.

"I was randomly selected, weren't you?" he answered.

"Randomly selected?!" Acara gaped.

"Yes. There are certain eligibility criteria according to Eirlon law, but the process of selection amongst the eligible candidates is random. This is how we select our leaders and government representatives as well. The random selection ensures that we have a fair representation of our whole population. Why, is it different for Humans?"

"You didn't compete to come to the Ring?" asked Acara incredulously.

"Why would we compete to go to our deaths?" Kael answered, equally incredulous.

"It's a great honor for us to be chosen to go to the Ring. We train almost our entire lives just for the chance to *compete* to go to the Ring."

"What a strange species you Humans are."

"Right, *we're* the strange ones," grumbled Acara. Kael looked at her inquisitively, as though confused by her sarcasm. "But, really, how do you expect to win the Ring if you don't train for it? Do you really think a random selection from your population maximizes your chances here?"

69

"Maybe you humans would understand better if you had lost as many to the Ring as we Eirlons have. We have been in hundreds if not thousands of Rings – you've been in, what, five or six? Many Eirlons have grown used to a nomadic life and not many are thrilled with the prospect of certain death. For Eirlons, it must be a lottery because no one in their right mind would volunteer anymore."

Acara sat and pondered Kael's perspective. She couldn't imagine a world in which not a single human would volunteer for the Ring.

"Well, if you were randomly selected to come here, what did you do on your ship before?" Acara inquired, even more curious about Eirlon life.

"I was a historian," Kael replied. "I studied the ancient history of the Eirlon people and our former planet of Eirlos. You Humans are relatively new to the Displaced, whereas we Eirlons have been Displaced for several millenia. While we have some historical records of Eirlos, much of the knowledge of how people used to live has been lost. My job was to put together the information gleaned from our ancient texts and hand-me-down stories and try to paint a picture of the life we once had."

"So what have you learned about the past, then?"

"Unfortunately, very little," sighed Kael wistfully. "Like all great civilizations, our greatest downfall was hubris. We believed that everything we created would give us more control over the world, over life itself, and we never thought that the things that gave us incredible power could also destroy us. Ancient Eirlons manufactured diseases and cures, machines that could kill and ones that could heal, instruments that could build and ones that could destroy utterly. In the end, each new discovery brought us closer to the brink of self-destruction until finally, inevitably, we built something so powerful that there was no counterbalancing it."

"What was it?" breathed Acara in fascination.

"That's the problem – our shame was wiped from all our records. No one knows anymore," said Kael. Acara goggled at him in disbelief and disappointment. She wondered if humanity could ever forget why it abandoned Earth.

*I hope not,* Acara thought. *What's that saying? Those who do not learn from history are doomed to repeat it?*

The pair lapsed into their usual silence again as they continued their journey. The leaves tinkled overhead like chimes and the soft ground squelched between their toes. They still had a long way to go.

*Chapter Fifteen*
*Axton*

Watching the Ring was a cruel and inescapable torture for Axton. Confined to his hospital ward, all Axton could do was stare helplessly at his holotube as the Intergalactic Council broadcasted live feeds from the Ring. Never in his life had he felt as feeble as when he watched Deimos threaten Acara's life, unable to protect her or help her in any way. Now, as he was forced to watch the Eirlon get closer and closer to Acara, he felt a new emotion beyond the desire to protect her – he felt jealousy.

The only good thing about being relegated to his hospital bed was the fact that the nurses made sure to keep the prying press away. Ever since Acara's ascension to Ring Champion, reporters had been pursuing Axton relentlessly in the hopes of getting his side of the story – no doubt eager to hear how Acara had sacrificed him for the chance to go to the Ring. Even without the press being able to access him, Axton had become an overnight celebrity within the Human Fleet. He had to admit his story was pure tabloid gold – orphaned at an early age, a promising start as a star Candidate, betrayed in the end by his own best friend.

He often thought back to the harsh sendoff he gave Acara at the Ring Banquet. Their interaction replayed in his mind over and over. The crushed look in Acara's eyes, the shiver of her bottom lip as she held back her emotions, the way she called his name as he turned from her – it made his chest hurt even more than the bullet wound that Acara had inflicted.

"How are you doing today, Lieutenant?" the Commandant strode into Axton's room without so much as a knock.

Axton muted the holotube broadcast.

"Better, sir," he replied, struggling to sit upright while not upsetting the intricate network of tubes and needles connected to his body. It took a lot of Fillers to heal the damage from the gunshot wound and he had to be pumped full of them all day.

The Commandant nodded in response, taking up a seat next to Axton's bed. His gaze fell to the silenced Ring broadcast, now showing two scaled aliens wading through shallow water. The image shifted to focus on another pair of aliens watching the first two, concealed in foliage along the beach. Of course, their presence was unbeknownst to the Ring competitors – only the people at home watching had the omniscient view of the situation. It was obvious what would happen next – someone would get eliminated.

"It's hard to watch, isn't it?" the Commandant remarked in a rare moment of empathy.

Axton knew that if anyone understood what he was going through, it was the Commandant. After all, the Commandant had lost his two best friends in the last Ring – he must have felt just as much futility watching the broadcasts then as Axton did now.

"Yes, sir. 90% of the Ring is hiking or fishing or some other mundane survival activity, but I can't tear my eyes away. I'm always afraid I'll miss the moment that something actually happens."

"You need to get some rest, regain your strength. You look like hell."

"Yes, sir."

A few moments passed as they both watched the scaled aliens walk straight into the ambush. Two more competitors down.

"Lieutenant, our senior leadership has asked me to name a Candidate to the Earth Council – someone who I think is capable of leading humanity in rebuilding Earth if we are successful in the Ring. Someone who I think is capable of rallying our cause if we are unsuccessful in the Ring. I am nominating you," the Commandant said without ceremony, always business-like.

"Sir?" Axton asked in disbelief. "I don't understand."

"If you'd bothered to watch any channel besides the Ring broadcast, you would know what's going on outside your hospital retreat. My decision to send two 'murderers' into the Ring as a representation of humanity was not exactly popular. There's been a real political backlash against the Candidate program, particularly my leadership of it. Your face has been plastered all over the news media as a poster child for all the good qualities of humanity. Apparently, your story resonates with society and people have been clamoring for more of you. You're a regular celebrity now."

"But I still don't understand."

"There's an opening on the Council now – because I have been 'asked' to step down. I'll still be Commandant of the Candidate program, but I will no longer sit on the Council or provide my input to political affairs."

"I'm sorry, sir."

"I'm not. I never liked politicians. Anyway, at least I am able to recommend my replacement, and given your performance in the Gauntlet and your general popularity, I think you would be an apt Councilor. So do you accept?"

"It ... it's an honor, sir," answered Axton sincerely.

The Commandant harrumphed in approval and stood to leave.

"Turn the broadcast off and get some rest – that's an order. I will inform the President of your decision ... Councilor."

Axton shook his head in disbelief. *Me, a Councilor?*

He'd always assumed that, if he never became a Ring Champion, he would follow the same career trajectory as every other

Candidate who graduated from the program – become a Fleet Officer. After all, Candidates were raised with the same military discipline as the soldiers in the Fleet. It was a natural fit. Sometimes, in idle reveries, Axton would imagine himself becoming a Lightjumper pilot or even the Commandant of the Candidate program. Never in his wildest dreams did he think he would hold political office, especially not one so high, so early.

Becoming a Councilor would be a huge burden of responsibility, but somehow Axton felt as though a weight was lifted from his chest. Maybe he didn't have the power to help Acara in the Ring, but he would have the power now to help humanity outside of the Ring, and that was something.

*Chapter Sixteen*
*Acara*

The past couple of days were a blur of hiking and sleeping and Acara was starting to tire. She counted herself lucky that the ground was soft and the air was warm, otherwise her lack of shoes and proper human clothing would have been a real problem. She also counted herself lucky to have Kael around. Even though he still limped on with a staff, he moved much more swiftly and elegantly than she imagined anyone could with a sprained ankle. His super eyesight had so far proven reliable - they hadn't seen any other competitors since the first day, although Acara didn't whether to credit Kael or pure luck for that.

Having the Eirlon around was proving useful in unexpected ways as well. Kael was the one who had found the edible berries the second day of their trek, which saved the pair from having to rely on their dwindling supply packs. Acara still didn't know how he could tell they weren't poisonous. The berries had certainly looked poisonous by human standards – little neon blue bulbs covered in red veins. She had watched Kael stuff a handful of the berries in his mouth, juices running down his chin, and even then she waited an hour before she could bear to try one. They were honeyed and tangy and delicious, and it was hard for her to wait another hour to test another berry. It was a sweet reward to cram a dozen in her mouth when she finally felt assured that Kael wasn't trying to poison her.

Kael had also been the one to kill the first indigenous fauna, a plump, floppy-eared pig-looking thing that he called a "Puglit." When Acara asked Kael where he got the name "Puglit" from, he said they had something like it on his home planet. "Irritating bouncing blob of fur" would have been a more appropriate name in Acara's opinion. She had tried to catch the Puglit but failed miserably as it kept ricocheting away in random directions. Kael was the one who was able to find the Puglit's nest and steal its eggs, but not before breaking the creature's neck as it hopped over to investigate. That night, Acara and Kael ate fried eggs and smoked the Puglit meat over a low fire so they could preserve it for later. After a few days of liquid meals, the chewy Puglit meat had tasted like heaven.

Even though Acara was starting to appreciate having the Eirlon as a partner, she still forced herself to be wary. They had traversed a great distance together, but mostly in silence on Acara's part. She was careful not to ask any more personal questions to Kael – after all, it would just make it more difficult to kill him later. But Kael didn't need questions. He did just fine thinking of things to talk about on his own. In fact, since the Ring broadcast, Kael seemed ready to share his life story. Acara wasn't sure if he was being calculating or if he just liked hearing his own voice.

"Look, here's another one!" said Acara, pausing to point at a large rock formation. It looked like a line of perfectly square cubes of quartz stacked around what used to be a square perimeter. Acara and Kael had passed similar ones in the past couple days but they seemed to pop up more frequently now that they were getting closer to the crystal spire.

"It's just a natural rock formation," sighed Kael for the hundredth time.

"You really think perfect cubes occur naturally?" asked Acara. She stared at the rock formation again. It looked almost like a building foundation.

"On this planet, maybe," said Kael.

Acara shook her head in disagreement but let it go. Kael had been surprisingly taciturn on the subject and she would figure out why eventually, but not today. The sun was going to go down soon and they needed to set up camp for the night. Tomorrow they would reach the spire and maybe she would press Kael for more debate in the safety of the summit.

"Let's camp here tonight," Acara suggested, setting her pack against a quartz block. Kael nodded and followed suit.

After setting up a few rudimentary perimeter alarms, the pair sat down to a meager meal of berries and leftover Puglit jerky and watched the sky darken. One thing about this planet was that the night never got as dark as Acara was used to on the spaceship. The twin moons were constant presences lighting up the night sky, casting pale beams through the silvery jungle.

Acara glanced surreptitiously in Kael's direction, waiting for the exact moment when the night sky would become dark enough to see his glowing violet eyes. She couldn't help but be mesmerized by the only thing that visibly set Eirlons apart from Humans. Over the past few days, Acara had noticed small things about Kael that made her even more curious about him. Unlike Axton, Kael didn't have the callused hands of a warrior or the practiced coordination of a hunter. He did, however, have an easy grace that marked his movements. His smiles were rare, unlike Axton who doled them out freely, and his face became placid in concentration, unlike Axton whose eyebrows furrowed. Yet, somehow, Kael reminded her of Axton.

"Who is he?" Kael asked abruptly, catching Acara staring at him.

"Who? What?" answered Acara, flustered. Could Eirlons read minds?

"Sometimes I find you looking at me as though I'm someone else," said Kael. "So who is it that I remind you of?"

"No one, you just look startlingly human, that's all," Acara lied, hoping to end the conversation.

Kael looked at her doubtfully.

"I had someone I loved as well before all of this," admitted Kael. He pressed on even as Acara opened her mouth to protest. "You don't need to deny it. I understand. It's hard to let go of someone even though you know you can't possibly keep them. Just remember – you can never truly lose someone who has loved you."

78

"I'm going to gather some more berries," announced Acara hastily, ending the conversation. "I'll be right back."

Before Kael could protest, she disappeared into the surrounding foliage, her cheeks red. Kael's words had made her inexplicably flustered. Putting Axton and the word "love" together in the same train of thought made Acara feel a mix of confusion and giddiness.

Acara stared into the night sky, imagining that the stars above were the lights emanating from the Earth fleet. She wondered what Axton must be thinking now, seeing her cooperating with the enemy. She imagined that "love" was probably the last thing he'd be feeling toward her.

The snapping sound of a twig breaking jolted Acara from her thoughts. Suddenly alert, she spun toward the source of the noise, straining to see in the dim light.

"Kael?" she whispered as someone stepped from the shadows.

"It's me," said a familiar voice. "Your partner."

Acara gasped and instinctively generated a Material Surge in the form of a blade, cursing herself for leaving her weapons behind at the camp. Deimos stood in front of her, his imposing form even scarier in the darkness.

Something was strange about him, though. The sneering expression that was normally on his face was replaced by something that looked strangely like kindness.

"I've found something that can help us. Come with me," he said, sounding as friendly and genial as anyone could.

*Either he's gone crazy or ...*

A sudden realization dawned on Acara.

"Ok, show me," she said as naturally as she could, moving toward Deimos.

He gestured for her to go ahead of him. She smiled sweetly when she reached him, pretending to follow his directions. Instead, she feigned left and came at Deimos with a swing of her biotic blade, burying it deep into his side. She twisted and felt cold blood wash over her hand as the Material Surge faded, leaving a gaping hole in Deimos's side.

The façade of Deimos warped and melted, revealing a dying gelatinous alien creature, its life pouring out of its body like a punctured water balloon. Acara watched its last shuddering moments and turned to leave, only to come face to face with Kael.

"How did you know that wasn't really your partner?" he asked, both suspicious and curious.

"How do I know that you're really you?" Acara retorted, backing up into a fighting stance.

Kael stepped aside to reveal a dead body behind him – it was the gelatinous mimic's partner, now reduced to an oozing blob impaled on Kael's walking stick.

"I should have seen their camera bubbles earlier – I'm sorry," Kael apologized, extricating his staff from the carcass.

Acara nodded, still regarding Kael with suspicion. She followed him back to camp warily, half expecting him to morph into another alien.

Kael didn't seem nearly as perturbed – he went straight to bed when they reached the camp. Acara watched the rise and fall of his chest as he drifted into sleep, not daring to let her guard down until his breathing had been even for almost an hour.

Eventually, Acara fell into a restless slumber. It was impossible to tell where her dreams of Axton ended and her dreams of Kael began.

### Chapter Seventeen
### Kael

Kael awoke with a hand clamped down hard on his mouth. He opened his eyes to see Acara's face inches from his own, her finger pressed against her pillowy lips in a signal to remain quiet. Kael followed her gaze and saw something that made his heart freeze. There were at least five camera spheres floating in the air not ten yards away from where Kael and Acara were pressed against the ground. Luckily, the rock formation had done a good job of hiding them from view, but it wouldn't be much use if the group got any closer.

The sky was beginning to lighten with the first hint of dawn, but it was still dark enough out that the group of competitors was hard to identify. Four of the competitors looked roughly the same size and build – lanky and humanoid – but the fifth had a strange silhouette that Kael couldn't identify. It had a large X-shaped frame with appendages growing arbitrarily from the ends. Two ovular bulbs extruded from the center of the X, bobbing independently of one another in a non-discernible pattern.

Kael felt the pressure of Acara's hand disappear and watched as she slowly and silently pulled three Sarlek-tooth daggers out of her pack. He'd had no idea Acara had more than one dagger this whole time and felt a little annoyed that she never entrusted him with one. The annoyance faded as he watched Acara strap one of the daggers to his staff, turning his walking stick into a spearing weapon.

Acara pointed to her eyes and then motioned towards the group of opponents, holding up five fingers to signal that she counted five enemies. Kael nodded.

*Too many*, Acara mouthed. Kael nodded again in agreement. He could see Acara's mind working furiously to come up with a plan.

The jungle was starting to fill with the reflected light of the morning sky, silver leaves illuminating the forest with the rising sun. It was too bright now to hope to sneak away without confrontation, but also bright enough that Kael could see the group in full, horrifying detail. The X-shaped alien that he couldn't seem to figure out earlier was actually two aliens fused together, creating a single angular monster with transparent skin through which every internal organ was visible. The ovular bulbs were the two heads of the aliens, which explained their disparate motions. Kael had read about the species of X-shaped aliens, Twinletteels, and how the males and females had to bond together or face a lifetime of handicap. It sounded to him like a bad horror story, but now it was right in front of him. The other two pairs of aliens looked very similar in the way that humans and Eirlons bore a strong resemblance. They walked upright and had humanoid features but were covered head to toe in bright gold scales. Kael guessed that the smaller pair were Gleemps and the larger pair were Yimmets, but it was impossible to tell for sure without seeing their tongues. Gleemps were supposed to have frog-like tongues that, when unfurled completely, were as long as a Gleemp's entire body. Yimmets had normal human-like tongues but had the physical strength of ten Gleemps. Somewhere along the line of evolution, Gleemps and Yimmets probably shared the same ancestor so it made sense to see them working together. The presence of the Twinletteel was a mystery, though.

"I'll lead them away. Take the packs and run for the spire. Don't stop," Acara murmured softly, her breath a velvety whisper that sent tingles down Kael's spine.

Kael wanted to protest but Acara was up and out of cover in an instant, a dagger in each hand. He watched as Acara hurled both daggers in the direction of the enemy. An enraged shriek pierced the air – clearly, Acara's daggers were right on target.

"Come get me!" Acara taunted, running east, away from Kael and away from the spire. Kael dared to peek around the stone formation and saw the glint of gold scales disappear into the woods after Acara. He also saw the two dead aliens lying sprawled on the ground – a Yimmet and a Gleemp – each with a dagger protruding from the back of its head. Kael was impressed. Not everyone, human or Eirlon, could throw with such precision, and ambidextrously no less. Some people, Kael included, were quite capable with weapons. Others were simply uncannily deadly with weapons and Acara clearly fell into that category.

As soon as the coast seemed clear, Kael pulled the daggers from the corpses with a sickening squelch and put them in Acara's pack. He set off at a quick pace toward the crystal spire, leaning on his spear for support. He knew it must be close. The crystal of the spire let off a UV glow that his special eyesight could see from a hundred miles away. Every step closer, the light from the spire grew stronger.

A half hour passed and Kael started to worry. He knew Acara was capable of handling herself, but she had at least three aliens chasing her. Who knew if she would run into others. Kael cursed himself for not stopping her. Three on two weren't terrible odds – they could have taken out the remaining aliens together. Or he could have at least followed after Acara and speared one of the aliens behind her. But no, he had let a small, human ... girl, really, run into the jungle with aliens trying to kill her chasing behind.

*What kind of Eirlon am I*, Kael berated himself silently as he cut through the forest undergrowth.

The glow of the spire was so strong now that Kael had to squint as though he were looking into bright sunlight. He was lucky it was still early morning – the light from the spire would be unbearable in full daylight. Kael emerged from the trees into a clearing in front of the spire, his breath catching as he witnessed the monument in its full glory for the first time. The shimmering spire was hewn from a single block of purple crystal, cut in such a way that a myriad of small facets caught every drop of light. Its peak rose high above the forest canopy, its pinnacle a jagged point against the rose pink sky.

A stir of emotions welled up in Kael at the mesmerizing sight. Happiness, elation, and excitement, fought with fear, regret, and sorrow to dominate Kael's heart. He'd made it to the spire, but somehow, it didn't feel right without Acara. After all, the girl had saved his life twice now. Maybe that didn't mean anything to humans, but to an Eirlon, it meant everything.

*I don't even know if she still lives,* Kael suddenly thought. The idea burned in his chest and he would have carved it out with a knife if he could have.

Kael shook himself out of his daze as he tried to focus on the spire and the real reason he had come in the first place. All the answers he sought lay within the spire, and he had to find a way in. With or without Acara.

It didn't take long to find the entrance even though the smooth archway of the door was built almost seamlessly into the base of the spire. However, it took considerably longer to figure out how to get the door to open. Kael tried pushing the door inward and sliding it to the side, but to no avail. He looked for some sort of keyhole or lever that would open it. The surface of the entry was covered with the same precision facets as the rest of the Spire and each looked identical to the other. Was he supposed to press on them in some sequence? Kael leaned his face closer to the door so that he could examine its pattern more closely. As soon as he did, a bright light blinded him as a beam radiated from the door and scanned his retinas.

The light abruptly disappeared and Kael waited. Nothing happened. Just as he decided to try again, a groaning sound emanated from the spire. It seemed to Kael that the whole monument pulsed with energy for just a millisecond before the panel of crystal before him slid open, sinking into the ground. The entrance revealed a hollow chamber with vaulted ceilings within the spire, reverberating with the residual hum of some sort of energy source. The entire room was filled with the light gathered and reflected by the translucent purple crystal walls, glowing from within like some ethereal dimension. In the center of the chamber stood what looked like a shallow circular pool made of white marble, filled to the brim with viscous silver liquid.

The inner sanctum of the spire held all the answers that Kael had sought all along. It was proof positive that his suspicions were correct and he had not risked his life in vain in the Ring. Still, Kael hesitated at the doorway. *Come on, Acara, where are you?* he pleaded silently. Kael sat down next to the entrance, resting his back against the cool crystal wall. Everything he had hoped for was just footsteps away, waiting to be discovered. And yet, he waited.

*Chapter Eighteen*
*Acara*

Acara was running out of stamina. Her heart hammered in her chest as she sucked in breath after breath, trying to force herself to keep running. Behind her, a huge, angry alien was closing in, its charging steps shaking the ground as it gave chase. It was one of the aliens that Acara had seen on the Intergalactic Council ship but didn't recognize – the giant tank-like creatures covered in hardened plates. The aliens were even more formidable now that Acara realized they weren't just big and seemingly invulnerable, but also surprisingly quick on their feet.

*This wasn't part of the plan,* Acara thought ruefully.

It had been too easy luring the Gleemp, Yimmet, and Twinlettels away and toward the traps that she had carefully set up during the long hike to the Spire. What she hadn't anticipated was running almost directly into the tank creatures as she fled from the other aliens. The tanks looked just as surprised as Acara did as she sprinted right through the middle of their camp. Luckily for Acara, the tank aliens recovered from their surprise just in time to deal with the other aliens that were following in her wake.

Hazarding a backwards glance, Acara witnessed one of the tank aliens deal a crushing blow with its armored fist to the Gleemp's head. Blood, bone, and glimmering gold scales sprayed outward from the alien's destroyed face in a shower of instant death. But Acara had barely noticed that part – she was more focused on the other tank who had evidently picked up her trail. Acara ran even faster.

Now, the light emanating from the spire was visible through the trees and Acara only had a little farther to go. If she could only make it to Kael, they might have a chance of killing the tank alien together. Assuming he had made it to the Spire in the first place. And assuming he hadn't taken the opportunity to get away from Acara. And assuming he was willing to risk his life to help her.

The trees started to thin and Acara could see into the clearing surrounding the crystal spire. The spire itself seemed to pulse lightly with a luminescence she hadn't remembered seeing on her descent down to the planet. Normally, that might have concerned her, but she was too preoccupied with another problem – there was no sign of Kael anywhere. Her heart sank even more as she cleared the trees and ran through the open grass toward the spire, realizing as she got closer that the formation was too smooth to climb. *So much for plan B*, thought Acara.

"Acara!" a voice called out. "Over here!"

Acara had never been so happy to hear her name. She looked toward the sound and saw Kael standing in the shadows of some sort of crack at the base of the spire, a crack that began to look suspiciously like a door as Acara's perspective on the spire shifted. He held a spear in one hand and waved the other one wildly from side to side as though unsure if Acara had seen him.

With a last burst of adrenaline-fueled strength, Acara booked it towards Kael. The stitch in her side throbbed while her legs burned with the effort. Her quick pulse boomed in her ears, barely overpowering the sound of the thudding footsteps pursuing her. She was close enough to see Kael's glowing purple eyes now and that he was, in fact, standing inside a doorway of some sort. He had tossed aside the spear for some unfathomable reason and stood, simply waiting, for Acara.

*I hope he has a plan,* Acara thought doubtfully, *a better plan than throwing aside his only weapon and waiting.*

Acara panicked as she noticed the doorway beginning to grow smaller as though sealing from the bottom up. Kael continued to yell unintelligibly at her, motioning frantically for her to hurry. With one last biotic surge, Acara launched herself over the threshold of the doorway, crashing directly into Kael. They landed together on the floor in a painful jumble of limbs, the impact knocking the wind out of both of them. As Acara struggled to regain her breath, she watched the door seal behind her even as the tank alien hurtled into it with the full force of his armored might. Whether the resounding crack she heard was the tank's exoskeleton or the crystal itself breaking, Acara couldn't be sure. But it didn't matter now – she was safe.

"Are you hurt?" Kael asked Acara, grimacing from her elbow digging into his abdomen.

Acara rolled off of him in response, still struggling to breathe normally and lower her heart rate. She rested her head for a moment against the stone floor, savoring the cool feeling against her burning skin.

After a little while, Acara recovered enough to take her first serious look at her surroundings. She was in some sort of light filled chamber where the only object inside seemed to be a round pool in the middle of the room. The silvery liquid in the pool threatened to overflow, its meniscus bulging above the rim of the container. Acara took a moment to stare in wonder but her thoughts quickly turned to Kael. In a flash, Acara was on her feet, grabbing the spear on the ground in one smooth movement and putting its sharp tip between herself and Kael.

"What is this place?" Acara snarled, instantly on guard. "Why did you bring me here?"

"You don't need to point that spear at me. I'm not going to hurt you," said Kael.

"Like you could," Acara answered haughtily.

Kael approached Acara, his hands open and held out to his sides in the most non-threatening gesture he could muster. His eyes never left hers, even as she glared back at him with a look of anger and hurt. He stopped in front of Acara, the tip of the spear she held pressing gently into his chest.

"I'm sorry I deceived you. I needed your help to get here and I didn't think you would help me if I told you the truth," admitted Kael.

"Start. Explaining."

"This place," sighed Kael, motioning around the room, "is one of many monuments built to preserve the memory of a great and ancient civilization that once inhabited this planet. It is a repository for all the knowledge that this civilization once held."

"How do you know this?" Acara asked with a lump in her throat, already anticipating the answer.

"Because this planet ... is Eirlos."

Acara should have been surprised, but she almost felt a sense of validation. She thought back to the signs – the giant steps on the beach, the ruins she and Kael camped at the night before, Kael's uncanny knowledge of the planet's indigenous wildlife. Even the color of the crystal spire itself was eerily similar to Kael's eye color.

"I guess that means you weren't randomly selected to come here then," said Acara with an edge to her voice.

"No. I volunteered."

"Did you always know this was Eirlos?"

"We suspected but did not know for sure."

"How could you not know your own home planet?" asked Acara incredulously.

"You must understand, we abandoned Eirlos several thousands of years ago. We never thought to return again. Many of the records of Eirlos have been lost or damaged or purposefully altered over generations. And much has changed on this planet since we left. Nature has reclaimed all of our great cities and metropolises. The topography of the land is all but unrecognizable and all that remains standing of our civilization are these spires. When the Intergalactic

Council made the announcement about finding this planet, we had not the slightest inkling that it may be Eirlos. It was only upon seeing the spires that we began to suspect. I swear this to you."

"I don't believe that an entire race could forget where they come from."

"I can prove it to you. Will you let me show you?" Kael asked.

Acara looked back at him doubtfully, but eventually lowered her spear. She nodded.

Kael walked over to the far side of the pool and placed his hands over a marble console that Acara had previously overlooked. The console was studded with crystals of various sizes that shone brighter as Kael's graceful fingers passed over them. As the crystal sequence progressed, the silver liquid in the pool began to coalesce into a more solid form until a circular disc floated directly above the basin. The disc expanded until it was more than ten feet across, forming a hovering platform in the center of the chamber.

"Please, onto the lift," Kael said as he stepped onto the platform and held his hand out for Acara.

With a sense of trepidation, Acara allowed him to help her up. Kael said something in the Eirlon language that Acara didn't recognize and immediately the platform started to rise, propelled by some invisible force. Looking up, Acara could only see a solid ceiling of crystal. She wondered where the lift would take them.

It took almost a full minute for the lift to cover the several hundred feet to the apex of the spire. Once it was almost to the top, the lift locked into place, forming a new chamber out of the hollow cavity at the tip of the monument, with the platform as its floor. The crystal at the summit of the spire was translucent, as though it were so thin that it became see-through. The sheer walls formed a three-sixty degree window through which Acara could see for miles around.

"Well, you weren't lying about the view," commented Acara as she spun, admiring the scene of the forest below. From the great height of the spire, she could see the beach she had landed on and the slowly converging blue boundaries of the Ring.

"Nor am I lying about this planet being Eirlos," Kael said. He lay his palm flat against the crystal wall and spoke another word Acara had never heard before. The crystal began to shimmer, wispy lines appearing and melting together to form an image that took Acara's breath away.

Instead of a vast silvery forest, Acara looked through the crystal window and saw a sprawling city buzzing with activity. Great domed buildings stood out amongst a sea of marble houses. Elevated highways crisscrossed through the metropolis like ribbons around a gift. Spherical vehicles moved along the roads and zipped through the air from point to point. In the distance, long, narrow ships bobbed in the bay. Everywhere, small ghostly figures could be seen bustling about.

Acara was so engrossed in the illusion that she started at Kael's voice.

"This is Eirlos as it was at the height of its glory," Kael said, a twinge of pride mixed with the sadness in his voice.

Even as he spoke, the scene started to change rapidly like a video on fast forward. Acara struggled to follow the chaos that seemingly appeared from nowhere –explosions erupted throughout the city, ghostly figures fought openly on the streets, bodies piled up in alleyways, ships keeled in the water and sank. Eventually, a fog settled over the city and all became still – not with the stillness of peace, but the stillness of death. The fog began to consume everything it touched. Bodies in the streets rapidly crumbled into dust, followed by the buildings and homes, eroding as quickly as sandcastles in the tide.

Eventually, the fog began to clear and the first sprouts of nature began to take hold in the ruins. Trees shot up from the ground, spreading until all signs of the destroyed civilization disappeared under a blanket of silvery foliage.

"It was beautiful," Acara breathed.

"Yes. It was," replied Kael.

"That fog – what was it? Was that the reason your people left Eirlos?"

"I ... I don't know. It has never been mentioned in any of our historical records."

"So what happens now?"

"I don't know that, either."

Acara let the moment slip into silence, unsure of what to say next. Regardless of the planet being Eirlos, they were still in the Ring, still in the competition. Survival needed to be their first priority.

*My first priority*, Acara corrected herself inwardly. *Kael is not really my partner – he is, in the end, still my enemy. And this planet being Eirlos, I need to be even more cautious around Kael.*

But, Acara couldn't cement her resolve against Kael. Everything she had just seen and learned had affected her profoundly, changed something in her heart, but she wasn't sure how. All she knew was that everything was different now and it would never feel the same again.

## Chapter Nineteen
### Axton

"Eirlos? How could the Intergalactic Council not have foreseen this?" the Earth President demanded, pounding his fist on the podium in frustration.

"I assure you, Mr. President, that the Council had no idea," replied one of the representatives, literally ruffling her feathers in discomfort.

"That is no less concerning," President Roland spat in disgust.

The immense Council chamber reverberated with the voices of thousands of representatives reacting to the Earth President's words. The President looked around defiantly, standing in the center of the amphitheater with the other Displaced representatives. It was an intimidating position to be in, surrounded on all sides by landed Council species, but the Displaced parties looked unimpressed.

Axton stood with some effort, wincing as his chest muscles tightened. Though the Fillers had superficially healed his wound, his underlying muscles were still being repaired at the cellular level. The hospital had only discharged him a couple days ago and he was already dealing with crises after crises in his new role as Earth Councilor. He was glad to have the distraction – it saved him from being glued to the holotube, trying to catch whatever glimpse of Acara he could. But this extraordinary summit of the Council and Displaced was of utmost importance, both to humanity and to Axton in particular.

"What happens now?" asked Axton civilly, trying to get the conversation back on track.

"The Ring plays out as it will," the representative replied, her colorful plumage twitching with her response.

"Like hell it will!" the Eirlon Chairman protested, standing up so quickly that he knocked over his chair. "Eirlos is *our* home. There is enough substantiating evidence to support our claim to the planet. You must put a stop to the Ring now!"

"I understand your frustration, Chairman Kolar, but I'm afraid it is not so simple. Many lives have already been sacrificed in the Ring. The other alien species will not allow those sacrifices to be made in vain. You gave up your claim to the planet thousands of years ago. The Intergalactic Council will assign an investigative task force to examine the evidence you have compiled and then come to an official verdict thereafter."

The other Displaced representatives nodded in agreement, some staring at Chairman Kolar in guilt and others in anger. The Eirlon Chairman ran his fingers through his shockingly white hair. He knew as well as anyone that once the Council gave a decree, there was no appealing it short of open rebellion.

"All hope is not lost – you still have a competitor in the Ring, Chairman," another Council representative reminded him.

"A small consolation, when he is travelling with that scheming human," the Eirlon spat.

"Chairman, with all due respect, that 'scheming' human is the only reason your champion is still alive," Axton interjected heatedly. "You would do well to remember that."

The Eirlon looked from Axton to the Earth President, then back to the Council representatives, his eyes alight with fury.

"This is not over," the Chairman warned, stalking out of the room in distaste, his entourage following closely on his heels.

Axton sat back in his chair, emotionally and physically drained. He looked over at President Roland who looked every inch as weary as he felt.

"Sir, what should we do about this?" Axton asked, already anticipating the answer.

"We wait. We wait and hope that your friend Lieutenant Price knows what she's doing."

*Chapter Twenty*
*Kael*

Kael always knew the respite would be brief, but now that the moment had come to venture back into the arena, he wondered where the time had gone. For the last three days, he and Acara had holed up in the apex of the Spire with their packs of supplies and an amazing view of the Ring. They had slept enough to make up for all the other restless nights. When they weren't sleeping, they each stared silently out the crystal windows, Kael searching for camera bubbles and Acara searching for who knows what.

Over the past few days, Kael had tried to engage Acara in conversation and was met with polite but short answers. Ever since he had shown her the Spire's secret, Acara had been distant. She had given no reaction other than the single tear she shed after, and then it was like a door closed between her and Kael. Nothing he did could entice Acara to confide in him. Kael wondered what was going through her mind and whether he was wrong to have shared the burden of knowledge with her. The pressure Kael felt to survive the Ring seemed to multiply exponentially after learning that the planet was indeed Eirlos, until the crushing weight of it made him wake up every night in a cold sweat. He could only imagine what Acara must be thinking.

Although being inside the Spire gave Kael a sense of safety that he didn't look forward to relinquishing, a part of him was glad that the ever-shrinking Ring boundary was forcing them to leave. The Spire was starting to make Kael feel claustrophobic, as though he had to fight for space inside with the ghosts of his ancestors.

"Are you ready?" asked Acara, spear in hand and supply packs in tow. Her manner was crisp and businesslike as she handed a supply pack to Kael.

"Let's go," Kael replied as he dug a dagger out of his pack and held it ready in his hand.

The pair stepped blinking into the daylight as they left the Spire. The blue boundary of the Ring was glowing just at the edge of the far side of the Spire, continuing to move inward at a barely perceptible rate. Acara took the lead and Kael followed, looking from side to side for signs of enemies. The tank alien that had charged the Spire was gone, but something that looked suspiciously like a bony plate was left in the dirt. Kael saw Acara take notice of the plate, the corners of her lips turning upward in a hardly noticeable smirk.

Several uneventful hours passed as they hiked through the jungle in companionable silence. The pair headed east toward the beach they had originally landed on. From the Spire, Kael had seen a small island just offshore that would be an ideal defensible location. It had enough trees to provide adequate cover but not so many that it would be difficult to maneuver. Judging by the Ring's shrinking pattern, the island would have the added benefit of being close to where the boundaries would eventually converge. It was the perfect place to hunker down. Or, as Acara had joked in a rare moment of levity, it was the perfect place for a last stand.

As he walked, Kael struggled to make sense of his feelings for Acara. His brain told him she was his enemy, but his heart wouldn't allow him to look at her in that light. He couldn't overlook all the small kindnesses she'd done for him, even though they might have benefited her as much as him.

He thought back to the Spire, when Acara first saw Eirlos through the lens of the crystal. He pictured the rapturous wonder on her face and the infinite sadness in her expression as she watched the Eirlon empire crumble. It was as though, up until that moment, he had been seeing her in black and white – now, suddenly, everything was in color. Witnessing Acara's openness and vulnerability had triggered a protective instinct in Kael. At that moment, he had wanted nothing more than to gather Acara up in his arms and shield her from her own sadness. But that was days ago. There was no trace of that emotion on Acara's face now as she pressed through the forest.

Kael knew that Acara was just putting on a resolute mask, although he didn't know if it was for his benefit or the humans watching the Ring at home. The further Acara distanced herself from Kael, the easier it would be to kill him. Kael understood that much. But he didn't want to believe it.

### Chapter Twenty One
### Acara

Acara and Kael had taken refuge in a thick copse by the beach for the evening. It was as safe and secure as any makeshift camp could be, hidden by dense foliage and thickly intertwined branches. Acara was starting to hate feeling safe. Feeling safe meant that she didn't need to think about surviving, which meant that her mind wandered to other things. Things like her conflicting emotions about Kael and feelings for Axton.

It had taken a new level of willpower Acara didn't know she had to maintain her emotional distance from Kael over the last week. The journey back to the beach had been so peaceful that Acara found herself daydreaming about what it would be like to take a leisurely stroll through the woods instead of running for her life. To top it off, Kael was relentless in his kindness and understanding, making it especially hard for Acara to ignore him.

Kael. The thought of him made Acara feel wretched. It was easier when she had believed him to be some poor Eirlon who had the bad luck to be randomly sent to the Ring. Now that she knew that Kael was not only smart and kind and handsome, but also brave and determined, she found it hard not to want to get to know him better. There were a million questions she wanted to ask him but they would only lead her down a path of no return.

Acara's thoughts turned guiltily to Axton. She had thought of him remarkably little since the Spire. It would be easy to attribute it to the constant stress of the Ring, but deep down inside, Acara knew that she simply hadn't yearned for him in the same way lately. She wondered if he was watching her right now on his holotube, still hating her for what she had done to him. A couple weeks ago, Acara would have done anything for Axton's forgiveness. Now, it almost seemed easier if he hated her forever. At least that way, he wouldn't get hurt again.

Acara jolted out of her reverie as a holographic update lit up the night sky, the sixth in the past week. She wasn't surprised to see that more than eighty percent of the contestants were blotted out from the list now. As the Ring grew ever smaller, so did the number of survivors. She scanned the faces, knowing before she even arrived at his picture that Deimos was still alive. Someone as sick and twisted as Deimos didn't die easily.

Acara felt Kael's eyes on her and she turned to see him studying her face.

"What?" she asked warily.

"Every update, I see you searching for your partner's picture. And when you find it, I see fear and hate flash across your eyes," Kael observed. "That night by the ruins, you killed a mimic of your partner without hesitation, like you didn't care if it was him or not."

Acara remained silent, but Kael pressed on.

"I think we've been working together long enough that you can tell me what happened to your partner," coaxed Kael.

"We decided that splitting up would increase both our chances for survival," Acara answered vaguely. *Well, it isn't a lie,* she thought.

"Would he kill me if we ran into him now?"

"Of course," replied Acara.

*He'd kill me, too,* she added silently in her head.

"Would you let him?" Kael looked at Acara intently.

"Of course," laughed Acara.

"I'm not joking."

Acara found Kael looking into her eyes for an answer, and in his eyes, she saw something like anxiety mixed with hopefulness.

"Of course I would let him kill you," said Acara firmly after some thought. Kael looked crestfallen with her answer.

"Oh."

Kael fell quiet and Acara felt somehow guilty. After a few minutes of prolonged silence, he lay down on the soft grass and went to sleep, turning his back on Acara. Sighing, Acara followed suit, shutting her eyes against the awkwardness of the conversation.

*I'd let Deimos kill you because I don't know if I could do it myself,* admitted Acara silently as she drifted into sleep.

Chapter Twenty Two
*Kael*

The sun shone over the softly rolling waves, making the water shimmer like a mirage. Kael dug his toes into the soft sand of the beach as he searched for the island on the horizon. It was barely visible, a small stretch of black against the turquoise sea.

He glanced over at Acara who was preparing for the swim with a series of stretches that seemed designed to make Kael's heart race. She seemed unaware of the suggestive nature of her poses, which made Kael all the more entranced. He forced himself to stop gawking at Acara and put on his supply pack, securing a dagger to the outside of his thigh for easy access. Kael then walked straight into the ocean, wishing that the water was just a little colder.

"How far do you think it is?" asked Acara as she waded out to join him.

"No more than an Earth mile," Kael replied.

Soon, they were deep enough that the water was as high as Kael's chest. Acara was already treading.

"Race you there!" said Acara, taking a lungful of air. She started freestyle sprinting before Kael could respond.

Kael smiled at Acara's sudden upswing in mood. He could easily see that competition brought out the best in her. Hastily, Kael followed in Acara's wake, determined to catch up.

Acara was a strong swimmer, but Kael was better. His elongated strokes helped him sail through the water and in a few minutes, he was able to get close enough to reach out and pull on Acara's leg, dragging himself alongside her. Through the pristine water, he could see Acara scowl at him before she wrestled out of his grip and bolted ahead with renewed vigor. Kael allowed her a head start before he chased her again.

As Kael closed in for a second time, he was distracted by something shiny in the depths of the water. He peered into the gloomy depths, the salty ocean water stinging his eyes, and saw a glowing orb in the dark recesses of the ocean floor.

"Acara!" Kael shouted as he surfaced. He couldn't get her attention, though. She was still sprinting headlong toward the island, oblivious.

Kael ducked under the water again. There were now two orbs glowing faintly in the water but getting brighter by the second. They looked strangely familiar, but he couldn't quite place why.

As the orbs started to rise to the surface, Kael suddenly realized what they were. A sudden feeling of dread enveloped him. The glowing orbs were camera bubbles. And they were headed in Acara's direction.

With all his power, Kael sprinted towards Acara. He silently willed her to keep sprinting toward the island, but he could see the glowing camera bubbles closing in on her. Kael pushed himself harder. The camera bubbles were now moving parallel to Acara through the water. Although the orbs were clearly visible, the aliens they were attached to were not.

Kael was beginning to think he might have made a mistake, when suddenly he saw Acara jerked under the water by an unseen force. He was close enough to see the bubbles of air escaping from her lungs as she thrashed about in surprise. Her arms were pinned to her sides as though something was wrapped around her. A flash of silver emanated from her clenched fist – Kael thought it was a dagger at first, but it glowed too brightly and flickered out like a light. Acara sank quickly, dragged down by whatever had her in its grips.

After surfacing for a quick breath, Kael plunged downward following the stream of bubbles released by Acara. In the gloom of the depths, Kael could see her still struggling fiercely to get free. But, before he could reach her, a solid mass plowed directly into his chest, almost knocking the wind out of him. Kael could feel rubbery tentacles reaching their way around his body, trying to immobilize him, but he couldn't see his attacker. Instinctively, Kael grabbed the dagger strapped to his thigh and jammed it where he felt the most pressure against his body. Instantly, the grip on him loosened and inky blood darkened the water around him. The blood outlined his attacker's body, making it suddenly visible in the water. Kael stabbed everywhere he could reach until he felt the last tentacles unwrap from his limbs.

Frantically, Kael searched the water around him until he found Acara. He could barely make out her body drifting listlessly on the ocean floor, anchored by the other alien's invisible tentacles. Her eyes were closed and no more air bubbles emerged from her slightly parted lips. In the eerie light of the ocean, her skin had taken on the bluish sheen of death. Kael's heart leapt into his throat in panic.

As he got closer to Acara, the camouflaged alien clamped its tentacles around him and attacked. Hacking, stabbing, and slashing, Kael wielded his dagger wildly but dangerously against his enemy. Soon, the water was once again polluted with black blood. Wrapping an arm under Acara's floating figure, Kael pushed off the sandy bottom and swam swiftly towards the surface.

Kael sucked in a lungful of air as he breached the water, pulling Acara with him. He was careful to keep her head above the surface as he struggled toward the island. Minutes passed by like hours as Kael used all his strength to get to land, his muscles screaming in exertion.

Finally, they were on land. Kael dragged Acara's lifeless body onto shore, collapsing beside her in exhaustion. Acara's eyes were half closed and unseeing, her once pink lips tinged with blue. Bending his ear to her mouth, Kael listened with desperate hope for a sign of life, but heard none. He checked her limp wrist for a pulse and felt nothing.

"Don't die!" demanded Kael, pushing against Acara's chest with interlocked hands until water began to leak from her mouth. Acara's head lolled from side to side with the force of Kael's pumping, but she showed no signs of consciousness. Bending down, Kael tilted Acara's chin up and clamped his mouth over hers, forcing air into her body. He repeated the pumping and breathing over and over again, not daring to stop.

He lost track of how long he had been trying to resuscitate Acara but he knew it had been too much time. Acara lay motionless as Kael stopped what he was doing. She looked so much smaller now to him, devoid of the vitality that made her seem larger than life before. Her wet hair formed a black halo around her still face and goosebumps covered her pale skin despite the warmth of the sun.

Kael bellowed in frustration and grief, a visceral and heart-wrenching sound emanating from the very depths of his soul. Acara's arms flopped lifelessly as Kael gathered her in his arms in a final embrace. He crushed her body against his, as though holding onto her form would mean holding onto her spirit. Salt water dripped from Kael's hair and rolled down his cheeks, mixing with fresh tears as he buried his face against Acara's cold neck.

"I'm sorry," Kael whispered as he lay Acara gently back down in the sand. As he brushed a tendril of wet hair from her face, a fresh wave of rage overtook him. It wasn't fair that she died the way that she did. It wasn't fair that he was still alive. It wasn't fair that he couldn't save her. She'd saved his life twice and he couldn't even return the favor once.

In anger, Kael brought his fists down hard over Acara's chest. Her whole body jerked with the impact. Acara's eyes suddenly snapped open as she gulped down her first gasping breath of air.

"Acara!" cried Kael, his voice thick with emotion. He pulled Acara into a sitting position so that she leaned against his chest, her head resting in the crook of his neck. Stroking her hair, Kael tried to sooth her as she struggled to regain a normal breathing pattern. Acara was only semi-conscious and seemed unaware of Kael's presence, but it didn't matter to Kael. She was alive.

Soon, Acara's breathing slowed to a regular pace. Kael held her close as she shivered in the warm sand, enveloping her with his muscular arms until her body started to relax. His face was close to hers when she finally opened her eyes.

"Acara," Kael said as he looked worriedly down at her.

A small smile graced Acara's lips. Her gaze was bright but unfocused as she lifted a hand to Kael's face.

"Axton," she murmured as her eyes closed and her hand dropped away. Acara drifted off into a deep sleep, oblivious to the world.

Jealousy and disappointment flashed through Kael's heart before relief washed all his conflicting emotions away. Acara was going to be fine. That was all that mattered. Whoever Axton was, he wasn't the one in the Ring with her. Kael was.

"I'm right here," answered Kael.

### Chapter Twenty Three
### Axton

"Axton."

Hearing his name spoken aloud had never felt so good. Axton replayed the scene again and again on his holotube, zooming in on Acara's face as she uttered his name. He leaned back in the plush leather chair of his new Councilor's office, feeling happier than he had in a long time.

*She does care,* he thought to himself.

Over the past few days, Axton had found it nearly impossible to watch the video footage of the Ring, both logistically and emotionally. Being a Councilor meant interminably long meetings with seemingly everyone in the Displaced Armada and the Intergalactic Council. There was hardly a spare moment between settling this dispute or negotiating that deal to watch the Ring, although he always got quick updates patched through his comm implant.

Even when he had the time to watch, Axton found it harder and harder to stomach the video. It wasn't the gruesome death scenes or long bouts of boredom that were so difficult – it was seeing Acara grow ever closer to that damned Eirlon. Every interaction, every conversation, caused a wave of pain and regret to wash through Axton's heart. He could see them bonding and he hated it.

And then today, becoming a spectator to Acara's watery near-death experience – Axton didn't think he could watch something like that again. Unconsciously, he had held his breath the whole time, breathing normally again only when Acara started breathing again. Axton couldn't help but be thankful that the Eirlon had been there to save Acara. Even so, the very act of saving Acara made Axton hate the Eirlon more.

*It should have been me. I should have been there.*

The only redeeming moment was when Acara finally regained consciousness and uttered his name. It was as if the dark shroud that had been suffocating him had finally been lifted. Now, more than ever, Axton was determined to make things right. He could only hope that Acara lived long enough for him to make amends.

## Chapter Twenty Four
### Acara

The twin moons of Eirlos were rising in the sky by the time Acara awoke. Her eyes fluttered open groggily as she tried to regain her bearings. The sand she lay on felt soft again her skin, but her head pounded agonizingly. Her mouth felt dry and her throat raw, as though she had tried to swallow flames before she fell asleep.

*What happened to me?*

The last thing Acara remembered was swimming toward the island and being suddenly pulled under the water by something. Everything after that was a blur of disjointed memories – she remembered thinking how beautiful the sun looked from the bottom of the sea, wondering why she couldn't move her arms, and seeing Axton's face. But that was impossible. Axton wasn't in the Ring.

*Kael!* Acara thought in alarm. *Where is Kael?*

Acara bolted upright, the pain her head throbbing as she moved. She took in her surroundings – she was pretty sure she was on the right island. It was really not much more than a sandbar with tall, wispy trees sprouting haphazardly from the center. Lurid green crablike creatures scuttled past her at the edge of the water. But it wasn't the environment that interested Acara so much as the fact that she was completely and utterly alone.

A mix of relief and loss hit Acara as she came to that realization. On the one hand, she was glad Kael was gone. It meant maybe she wouldn't have to fight him later. But on the other hand, she felt as though a part of her had been taken away. They had been through so much together in the Ring, his abandonment felt almost like a betrayal. She thought that she had meant more to him. Focusing on the hurt of Kael deserting her made her not think about the dreaded alternative – that somehow he had gotten himself killed.

Looking around, Acara spied her supply pack a few feet away, half buried in sand.

*At least he left me my supplies.*

Acara crawled over to the pack, unsure of her steadiness on her feet. Suddenly starving, she tore into a piece of dried Puglit and gulped down the fresh water she had stored in her bag. She knew she should be rationing the water, but it felt so good as it soothed her burning throat.

The night sky suddenly lit up with a holographic broadcast. Acara watched eagerly as the footage from of the recent killings rolled through the clouds, hoping to shed some light on what had happened to her since her blackout. In a minute, she got the answer she was looking for but hadn't expected.

The broadcast showed Kael underwater, hacking and slashing with a mercilessness that Acara would never have expected from him. The water around him turned black with blood as he killed a camouflaged assailant. Acara gasped at the next image – it was a closeup of her face, her skin gray and her lips blue, lying in the very sand she sat upon now.

*Was I ...?* She was afraid to voice the thought even in her own head.

Her heart surged with a feeling she had never experienced before as she watched Kael resuscitate her over the broadcast. The camera zoomed in on Kael's expression as he tried to save her life – one of suffering, determination, and ...

*Love?* Acara thought, incredulous and confused.

Although she had never been in love before, she had seen it enough times that she recognized that look. But she hadn't given Kael any reason to love her. Nothing she had done was to impress him. In fact, she had gone out of her way to remain detached and keep him at arm's length.

The broadcast ended with the standard list of remaining contestants in the Ring. There were only a handful of champions left. Acara's eyes darted to the set of purple eyes that stood out from the rest of the pictures. Relief washed over her knowing that Kael was still alive, but it was soon replaced with anxiety as her eyes landed on Deimos's picture. That he was still alive and had been traveling alone this whole time was further evidence of his prowess. Acara was not looking forward to the inevitable moment of their confrontation.

A sudden movement in the periphery of her vision caught her eye. Someone or something was surfacing from the water. She stiffened, her hand moving swiftly to her supply pack in search of her dagger. It was gone. Acara cursed silently. She tried to force a biotic charge to her hand but found herself too weak to muster anything. All she could do was watch as the mysterious form got closer to the island.

"Kael!" Acara breathed, surprised at the enormous flush of warmth that overcame her at the sight of him. The first thing she saw was his glowing violet eyes blinking salt water from his long lashes. His naked torso glistened with droplets of water as he strode into the shallows holding a supply pack in each hand.

Even though it made her head spin, Acara struggled to her feet and half ran, half fell in Kael's direction. He saw her and gave her one of his rare smiles, his white teeth offsetting the brightness of his eyes. Tossing the packs onto the island, Kael met Acara at the edge of the water. The warm waves lapped at their ankles as they stopped just shy of one another. For a moment, neither one knew what to say.

"I went back in the water to retrieve the supply packs from the bodies. I thought we might have need of them," said Kael awkwardly.

"I thought you left me," admitted Acara, her tone both relieved and accusatory.

"I would never leave you," Kael answered with certainty. The conviction in his statement sent a shiver through Acara's entire being.

Another moment of awkward silence passed as both parties struggled to put words to their thoughts.

"Thank you for saving me," said Acara finally, other meanings imbued in her tone.

Raising her eyes to meet his, Acara was struck by the intensity in Kael's gaze. His purple eyes pulsed with a light that matched the rapid beating of Acara's own heart. Suddenly, his lips were on hers, kissing her with a gentle ferocity that shook Acara to her core. Kael wrapped his arms around Acara's waist as he pulled her towards him, pressing her against his body.

She could feel the ridges of his healing wounds as she rested her palm on his bare chest, kissing him back with all the unspoken emotions she felt.

"We can't," Acara hissed, pushing Kael away abruptly. She stepped back, her lips still searing from his kiss.

"I love you," said Kael plaintively.

"Obviously," said Acara, suddenly angry. "But you can't. So stop it."

"I don't understand."

"Don't you get it? Only one of us can survive the Ring. That means you can't love me. And you can't try to make me love you!" Acara cried. She was furious at Kael for making her emotions betray her, but more so, she was furious at herself for letting it happen.

"Acara, I'm sorry," placated Kael, reaching for her hand. Acara knocked it way.

"You should have just let me die!" Acara spat.

She brought her hand to her mouth in shock as though disbelieving the words that escaped from her own mouth. Acara quickly turned away from Kael, shaking at her own emotions. When she looked back, Kael had retreated to the other side of the island, leaving Acara alone with her thoughts.

*What is happening to me? A Ring champion would never say something like that. I would never say anything like that.*

A slow realization dawned on her at that moment, a feeling that she had been denying since the Spire. She wanted Kael to win. She wanted him to be able to restore Eirlos to his people. But most of all, she just wanted Kael to live. Now she finally comprehended why she had been pushing him away recently – not because it would be harder for her to kill him, but because she wanted to make it easier for him to eliminate her.

Acara shook her head as though trying to clear it of her treasonous revelation. Purposefully giving up in the Ring would be an epic betrayal of humankind in and of itself. But helping Kael win would mean helping him kill Deimos, a fellow human – an unforgivable crime. And now that the whole universe had seen her kiss with Kael, there would be no hiding her treason. She thought about Axton and what it would do to him to know that she had cost him his chance in the Ring and gave up her own, serving victory to another species on a silver platter. It made her heart ache.

Chapter Twenty Five
Axton

Axton sat once again in the center of the Intergalactic Council chamber with the President Roland and other Councilors by his side. The Eirlon Chairman and his party sat at the table next to theirs. Other Displaced representatives with champions still surviving in the Ring filled the other tables on the chamber floor. The Intergalactic Council representatives looked down at the Displaced, perched in their respective balconies circling the chamber floor.

"The Intergalactic Council calls to order the second extraordinary summit concerning planet XD-3011," the feathered representative in the center balcony began.

"Call it what it is – Eirlos!" one of the Eirlon representatives shouted.

A commotion arose from the other Displaced representatives.

"Order!" the Council representative demanded, her voice booming above all others.

The room quickly became quiet once more as every species eagerly awaited the Council decree. It was common knowledge that the Council's investigative task force had submitted its official findings only hours before this meeting. Everyone wanted to know what would happen next.

"Our task force has found that the Eirlons have submitted incontrovertible evidence that the planet XD-3011 is indeed their home world of Eirlos," the Council representative announced.

A cheer arose from the Eirlons and their supporters, although many more species stood silently awaiting the final verdict. It was obvious to most that the planet was indeed Eirlos – what mattered was what the Council decided to do about that fact.

"The magnitude of the decision at hand is not lost on us," the Council representative continued. "While this rare circumstance has never arisen before, it is possible, however unlikely, that it may arise again in the future. The decision we make here will set a precedent for all those that come after. In light of this fact and the sacrifices already made by the races of the Displaced, the Council has come to a unanimous decision. We decree that the Ring will continue until there is one clear winner. However ..."

The representative's voice was drowned out by the reactions of the other species. Through the din, it was hard for Axton to tell whether the uproar was in support of the decision or against it. Personally, he was torn. While it meant that humanity would still have a shot at winning the Ring, it also meant that Acara wouldn't be immediately and safely extracted. He looked over at the Earth President and found him leaning back in satisfaction in his seat. The red-faced Eirlon Chairman was shouting at the Council, spittle flying from his mouth.

Suddenly, all was quiet. Axton looked around – mouths were still moving and people were clearly still speaking, but it was as though someone had pressed a mute button.

"However," the council representative continued, "we recognize that the Eirlon species has a special claim to the planet of Eirlos. As such, the Council will support an equitable distribution of territories, should the Eirlons and other Displaced species with champions still remaining come to a unanimous agreement to end the Ring."

While the room was still artificially muted, there clearly was no need any more – all the Displaced seemed stunned into silence. Axton was shocked at the Council's announcement. He knew that the decision had implications far beyond the obvious, though what those implications might be were a mystery. All he could be sure of was that the decree had just ensured that he would have many more hours of meetings and negotiations in the near future.

### Chapter Twenty Six
### Kael

Days passed in uncomfortable quiet as Acara and Kael studiously ignored one another. During the sunlight hours, they set traps and built fortifications, exchanging words sparingly. At night when the twin moons rose, they sat on opposite ends of the island, picking at the meager meat inside the verdant crabs they caught during the day. All in all, it was a subtle torture for Kael to have to endure.

Today was passing in much the same manner. Kael sat whittling the end of an indigo branch into a sharp point, another javelin to add to the beachhead defenses. He glanced surreptitiously at Acara, watching the beads of sweat drip from her forehead as she dug another row of protective trenches around the perimeter of the island. Even though she was several hundred feet away, Kael's superior vision allowed him to catch every grimace on her face as she plugged away. Not once did she look up in Kael's direction.

Maybe avoidance was an acceptable coping mechanism for humans, but Kael couldn't accept it. The silent treatment was driving Kael crazy – from frustration to despair to anger. He'd given her a few days to cool off and come around, but it hadn't worked. It was time to try something else.

Kael stuck his javelin into the sand and walked purposefully towards Acara, sweeping his hair back subconsciously. He wasn't treading softly, so he knew that Acara's refusal to acknowledge his approach was willful and somehow that enraged him more.

"Acara, this cannot go on. I know neither of us is in an ideal situation – you especially. I know that what has transpired between us has been … unusual and surprising. But I also know that what we have is *good*. We shouldn't be acting like something is wrong between us. In this crazy situation, isn't what we have the only thing that is *right*?"

Kael caught his breath as Acara finally made eye contact with him for the first time in days. Her face was streaked with sweat and sand, her lips chapped from dehydration, but she had never looked lovelier to Kael.

"I don't know what to say," Acara relented. "I ..."

She broke off and her eyes darted past Kael, the softness disappearing from her expression in an instant. He wheeled, not sure what to expect. It was just the telltale shimmer of the Ring update in the sky, the first one in days. Resigned, Kael turned to watch the broadcast, knowing full well that Acara wouldn't give him her attention until it was over.

Unlike all the previous broadcasts, this one did not show any footage of Ring deaths, nor did it show any of the remaining competitors' photos disappearing. *There must not have been any deaths in the previous days,* Kael surmised.

"Is that ...?" Kael asked in disbelief, unable to finish his question.

The broadcast now showed a circular map dotted with red stars. It was a map. And judging from the placement of the stars, it was a map showing everyone's location in the Ring.

"Well, that's new," Acara commented numbly.

"Looks like we made the right call," said Kael, examining the map. Of the eleven stars left on the map, theirs were the only ones on the island. The rest were concentrated along the beach, forced to its edge by the ever closing Ring boundary.

"Yeah, but there goes our advantage."

As Kael watched, two of the red stars on the map converged and one disappeared. It was obvious what that meant. He exchanged a look with Acara. The only stationary markers on the map were their own – others were clearly fleeing or giving chase, judging by their movements. Four more stars disappeared almost simultaneously as they converged with others. Now that everyone knew everyone else's position, it wouldn't be long before more competitors were snuffed out.

"They're in the water ... we don't have long," Acara remarked calmly, all business once again. "How are our defenses?"

"The beachheads will slow them down but they're certainly not impenetrable," answered Kael.

"Let's hope slowing them down will give us enough of an advantage ... Look!"

Kael's gaze returned to the sky and his eyes widened in shock. The other remaining stars were now in the water heading toward the island. But two of the stars were fast approaching – they would be on Acara and Kael in a matter of minutes. Kael swiveled in the direction that the competitors were coming from and could see camera bubbles bobbing in the wake of two streamlined waves.

"Only one species can move that quickly – arm yourself!"

Cursing silently, Kael followed Acara to the weapons cache they had been stockpiling over the last few days. He picked up a pike and strapped a supply pack to his chest to protect his vital organs and a dagger to his ankle for close combat. Acara did the same, only grabbing a bagful of sharpened quartz arrowheads rather than a pike. Kael wondered what good the small arrowheads would do against their opponents but he trusted that Acara had a plan.

"I think the aliens approaching are Gesari – they move so quickly that the human eye can barely track them. None of our traps will do any good – at their speed, the traps won't even trigger. We can only hope to get lucky – they're fleshy and vulnerable, kind of like Humans and Eirlons. It shouldn't take too much to bring them down, assuming we can touch them."

Using his telescopic vision, Kael was able to see that Gesari were not actually swimming – they were moving so quickly that they were skimming on top of the water. In seconds, they would be upon the beach.

"They're coming!" Kael warned.

"Don't let them get close to you, Kael. Be careful."

Kael turned to face Acara for a brief moment, but found her already focused on the incoming foes, her brows knitted in concentration. Her fist was clenched around a handful of arrowheads, a soft buzzing sound steadily building in her hand. Kael registered the silvery white glow of Acara's fist in wonder. She had never said anything about having biotic enhancements.

*Why would she hide her abilities from me?*

The Gesari had reached the beach, their spindly humanoid bodies glistening in the water. Their skin was a fearsome red with black markings, like poison dart frogs that Kael had once seen in an Earth encyclopedia. They maneuvered around the beachheads in a blur of motion that even his superior eyesight had difficulty keeping up with.

As the Gesari paused to look up at the holographic map, Acara unleashed a torrent of arrowheads in their direction without warning. The arrowheads launched from her outstretched fingers, powered by a biotic surge, travelling as fast as bullets. But the Gesari, hearing the projectiles' hissing approach, dodged the surprise attack with seeming ease. Acara launched another handful of arrowheads at the Gesari, this time propelled forward with even more force. Again, the Gesari darted out of the way.

She broke cover, launching a third and final wave at the Gesari. This time her aim was true. One of the Gesari faltered and clamped a hand against its neck. Kael watched as black blood as thick as syrup oozed through the Gesari's long fingers.

"Finish it!" Acara yelled at Kael. She was sprinting in the direction of the unharmed Gesari at superhuman speeds, a dagger in each hand, her entire body enveloped in a silver aura crackling with energy.

Time seemed to slow down as Kael ran for the wounded Gesari. Although he tried to focus on his target, it was hard from him to tear his eyes away from the deadly whirlwind of static charge that Acara had become. He realized suddenly that he had never seen Acara in this light – her body was made for killing, that much was clear now. And she had kept her full capability hidden from him, as though she still viewed him as an enemy. The very thought made Kael feel foolish.

*No time for hurt feelings*, Kael berated himself.

He stabbed at the wounded Gesari as soon as he was in range, thrusting his pike forward at its chest. Even badly hurt, the Gesari was able to move deftly out of reach. Kael went in closer for the kill, this time aiming for the abdomen. The Gesari dodged the main thrust of his attack and latched onto the pike with its free hand. It yanked hard and Kael stumbled forward on his own momentum, almost losing his balance. A tug of war ensued as Kael tried to knock the Gesari off its feet. The Gesari was surprisingly strong given its waifish stature and proved as immovable as a tree rooted in the ground.

In the blink of an eye, the Gesari was within inches of Kael's face, moving at lightning speed. It clamped one hand and then another around Kael's neck, lifting him off the ground. Kael scrabbled at the Gesari's slimy skin, trying to pry its hands loose. He could see the blood pumping out freely from the Gesari's neck now that its hand was no longer staunching the flow, but the Gesari's grip belied no weakness.

The edges of Kael's vision began to turn red and he struggled for air. He felt himself weakening. Kael's fingers clawed fruitlessly at the Gesari as it tried to squeeze the life from his body. Just as Kael was about to lose consciousness, he felt the Gesari's grip weaken – it wasn't much, but it was something. He realized that his fingers had found purchase in the Gesari's bleeding neck wound. Kael's numb hands could barely feel the Gesari's hot blood running over them, but he forced himself with his last resolve to dig into the wound, prying it apart like the shell of a clam.

With a thud, Kael dropped to the ground, his legs buckling under. The Gesari stumbled backward as blood shot like a geyser from the massive gash in its neck. As Kael's vision started to come back, he could see the Gesari drop dead on the sand in front of him, its face contorted in pain.

Throat burning, Kael tried to force himself to his feet, using the pike for support. Several feet away, Acara was still fighting the other Gesari, matching it blow for blow at such a speed that Kael couldn't tell who was winning and who was losing. Whatever was happening, they were getting closer and closer to Kael.

"The pike!" Acara bellowed, her voice frantic. The silver charge around her was fading. Kael could tell she wasn't moving as quickly as she had been a moment ago because he could actually see the outline of her body instead of one big blur. There was blood dripping down her arms and face, and it wasn't black.

The effort of hoisting the pike almost made Kael black out again but he forced himself to stagger forward. With one last burst of energy, Acara assaulted the Gesari, driving it back towards Kael. Her relentless onslaught seemed to catch the alien by surprise as it backed away rapidly.

Kael felt the impact of the Gesari's body on his pike before his eyes could register what had happened. The shock of it made Kael drop the pike, but the damage had already been done. Impaled on the end was the Gesari, whom Acara had maneuvered straight into the point. With one last gurgling breath, the Gesari slumped to the ground, defeated.

Acara fell to her knees, breathing hard. The silver aura around her fizzled, leaving behind only a vulnerable-looking girl in the sand. Kael rushed to Acara's side, alarmed at how much blood he saw now that she was no longer cloaked in biotic energy.

"I'm fine, I'm ok," panted Acara, waving Kael away.

"You're bleeding ... a lot."

With a sharp intake of breath, Kael noticed the main source of blood – a stab wound in Acara's side that went all the way through to her back. Acara looked up, noticing Kael's reaction. She moved to cover the injury but winced in pain.

"It's just a flesh wound," Acara tried to reassure Kael. "Damn Gesari disarmed me and stabbed me with my own dagger. Cut some fabric off the Gesari's clothing so I can bandage it."

Kael did as he was told, but not without concern. He knew enough about human biology to know that so much blood loss would not be taken in stride, even if Acara was biotically enhanced. Gingerly, Kael pressed a folded square of fabric stripped from the Gesari against Acara's side. Acara let out a hiss of air and nodded at Kael to continue. He wrapped another piece of fabric around her slender waist and tied it tight against the wound.

"Can't you stop the bleeding like you did for me?" Kael asked, watching in anxiety as the fabric quickly became wet with blood.

"I could, but it would take away my full range of motion," answered Acara.

"Why do you need ..."

"Don't you see?" asked Acara, looking up at the sky. The holographic map was even smaller now, as the Ring boundaries tightened faster and faster. There were only three red stars left on the map – Kael's, Acara's, and one unknown red star in the water, moving on a straight trajectory to the island.

"He's coming."

### Chapter Twenty Seven
### Acara

Her whole body hurt. She felt drained from her fight with the Gesari, having pushed her biotic powers to their very limits. Every inch of her skin tingled with residual energy and her hands felt like they were rusting away. Acara wasn't even sure that she could summon another biotic pulse if her life depended on it, and it probably did.

Kael didn't look too fit to fight, either. He sat heavily in the sand, his arms behind him, propping him upright. Angry bruises circled his neck and the white of one eye had turned red with broken blood vessels. Acara longed to brush the sand and sweat-slicked hair out of Kael's eyes, but couldn't seem to muster enough energy. Instead, she collapsed her knees to the side and rested her head on Kael's shoulder. She felt Kael's posture stiffen in surprise and then relax as he pressed his cheek against her hair.

The pair rested in that same position for what seemed like a very long time. But the moment that Acara had been dreading was almost here. All she could do was wait.

Though he wasn't yet close enough to the island to see, Acara was sure that it was Deimos heading her way. Deep down inside, Acara had known that this would be the final battle. Axton would have called it "destiny."

*Axton.*

It seemed like such a long time had passed since she last thought of him. A pang of yearning crossed her heart – she wished Axton were there to give her advice. He would know what the right choice was. She could imagine him berating her, telling her that it was so obvious – she needed to kill Kael and claim Eirlos for humanity.

Acara sat up and turned toward Kael, her eyes locking with his.

"Kael – I ... I can't kill you," she said.

"Why do you say that like it's a bad thing?" asked Kael, the corners of his mouth twitching as though suppressing a smile. Acara could read the relief and happiness in his pale purple eyes and she hated herself for what she was about to say next.

"I can't kill you, but I can't help you, either. I can't kill Deimos. He's a fellow human. I ... I don't want to betray my entire species. Even if ... I have feelings for you," she ended lamely. She searched Kael's inscrutable expression for a sign that he understood.

"And what if I win against Deimos? What happens when it's just the two of us left in this damned arena?"

*You won't win,* Acara thought morosely.

"I hope you win," she said aloud.

Taking Kael's hand, Acara pressed her lips to his fingers in a gesture of affection. Before he could do something to change her mind, she limped away toward the other side of the island.

*Don't look back, don't look back, don't look back.*

Acara repeated the mantra in her head, tears threatening to spill from her eyes. She had gotten as far as the tree line on the opposite side of the island before she heard Deimos's voice, sending shivers down her spine.

*Don't look back.*

Even though Acara could hear the sound of manic laughter and wood splintering, she hoped that the beachhead and trenches would be enough to slow Deimos down. She hoped that Deimos was tired from the long swim to the island and the other competitors he had to defeat along the way. She hoped that Kael would remember to use the traps they set to his advantage.

*Don't look back.*

Deimos' enraged scream pierced the air and Kael's battle cry followed. Acara covered her ears to drown out the sound of the battle. Screwing her eyes shut only made her imagine the fight in vivid detail in her mind. Every fiber of her being wanted to run back to the beach, to help Kael, to stop Deimos. But she fought the impulse, pressing her palms against her ears even harder.

*Don't look back.*

## Chapter Twenty Eight
### Axton

Every eye in the meeting room was glued to the holotube as the last and definitive moments of the Ring came ever closer. The representatives of the final remaining species still alive in the Ring sat around the semi-circular meeting table, silent and waiting.

They had been locked in endless negotiations for days since the Council decree came down, with species leaving the table as their champions fell one by one. Now, it was down to six species, all waiting in desperate anticipation as the final surprise element of the Ring was initiated – the map. The map was something that was never broadcast to the general public, a measure put in place to ensure a swift ending to the Ring after the number of champions fell below a certain number. In some previous Rings, where the view of the sky was limited, the map didn't even matter – in this Ring, with its clear vistas and easily navigable terrain, the map would be crucial.

Axton grimaced as he watched the first species fall victim to the exposure of its location. It was a quick death, one that seemed obvious and inevitable to the viewers watching. With a sigh, the representatives of the species left, leaving only five species at the bargaining table.

Within another few minutes, another species was gone.

"There are only four of us left. Surely we can come to an agreement now to end this Ring," the Eirlon Chairman piped up, his eyes still on the holotube. Axton imagined how frustrated he must be that all the hours spent arguing over the past few days had resulted in nothing. After all, every remaining species believed it would win the Ring.

"Dominar, you must see the wisdom of coming to a settlement," the Chairman Kolar beseeched the head of the Gesari party. "Gaining one-quarter of a massive planet is far better than gaining one hundred percent of nothing."

"I have full faith that my species will win," the Dominar answered arrogantly.

No sooner had the words left the Dominar's mouth than one Gesari met his end at the hands of the Eirlon champion. The other Gesari followed shortly thereafter, dispatched by Acara herself. Axton felt a rush of pride upon seeing her in action.

"Bet you wish you had made that deal when you had the chance, Dominar," the Eirlon Chairman goaded, a look of vindication on his face.

For a moment, Axton was sure that the Gesari Dominar would punch Kolar in the face, but the moment seemed to pass.

"There will be more Rings and more planets for us, Chairman," the Gesari replied smoothly. "There is only one Eirlos for you."

Without another word, the Gesari entourage exited gracefully and Axton silently applauded the Dominar's rebuttal.

"Let that be a lesson to you two," the Eirlon pointed at the Human President and the other remaining species' representative. "Perhaps it would be a good time to reconsider your positions, especially you Humans. Looks like one of your champions doesn't have much time left."

Axton's attention snapped back to the holotube as he heard the Chairman's words. He watched in horror as the video showed Acara's wound bleeding relentlessly, soaking first her hands and then the bandage she wrapped futilely around it.

"You forget that we have two champions, Chairman. No deal," the President Roland replied calmly. Axton forced himself to put on a veneer of confidence to match the President's tone, even though he felt sick inside.

"We would be willing to make a deal," the remaining species at the table interjected. Unlike the Humans and Eirlons, they had only one representative left alive in the Ring. The creature was at least fifteen feet tall with every inch of its body including its face covered in plates – Axton recognized it as the same species that attacked Acara at the Spire, but other than that, he had never seen its kind before.

"We are new to the Armada. There are only a few of my people left after the complete destruction of our home world. This is our first Ring. It would be a great honor and great relief for our species to end this with both of our champions' lives intact and a new home to settle."

The tank-like creature stretched out a rocky paw toward the Eirlon Chairman. He clenched it with both hands, smiling.

"Thank you, Ambassador. Your support means a great deal to us. Now, if you would help me convince the Humans to do the same, we can all end this godforsaken blood bath and ..."

The Eirlon stopped mid-sentence as he watched the scene on the holotube unfold, mesmerized. Deimos was squaring off with the one tank alien remaining in the Ring and it appeared that he was winning. He had leapt onto the back of the tank with one arm firmly lodged in a soft spot under its chest plate. It was hard to tell what Deimos was doing with his hand beneath the plate, but whatever it was, it was clearly causing the tank alien a great deal of pain.

"Human President, we implore you to come to an agreement and end this Ring," the Ambassador pleaded.

"When we are winning? I think not," the President replied. While Axton agreed with him, he was a little taken aback at his callousness.

A scene of carnage began to unfurl across the holotube. Deimos had ripped out some internal organ with his bare hands, wounding the tank alien in what looked like an unnecessarily painful way. When the creature collapsed, Deimos ripped off one piece of shield-like exoskeleton after another from its body until its soft underskin was exposed. He then used the alien's own plates to beat it into bloody submission, ensuring that the being was indeed dead.

Axton breathed a sigh of relief when the tank alien finally stopped moving – the brutal way in which Deimos had taken his time to kill the alien filled Axton with revulsion. Judging by the expressions on the other Earth Councilors' faces, everyone felt the same way. Some even looked apologetically at the tank Ambassador, but it was impossible to discern his reaction under the layers and layers of plates covering his face.

"We shall remember this the next time you need our aid, Human," the Ambassador growled after a moment of silence. He stalked out of the room, each step shaking the floor.

The Eirlon Chairman looked defeated as he sat back in his chair. The Earth President said nothing. Once again, all eyes turned to the holotube. The end was coming. All anyone could do was wait.

### Chapter Twenty Nine
### Kael

As Deimos emerged from the water, Kael felt a dread that he had not expected. Deimos was enormously tall by Human standards, his muscles rippling as he waded from the shadows. Somewhere along the way, he had tossed his Council-issued clothing by the wayside and was instead covered with the skins of dead aliens. A necklace of bones rattled around his thick neck as he tore through the beachheads with his bare hands, one clenching a shield-like plate and the other tossing large obstacles aside as though they were nothing. All in all, he made for an intimidating sight.

Seeing Deimos, it became very apparent to Kael why Acara didn't stay with her partner in the Ring. He was a monster.

As Kael assumed a fighting stance, pike in hand, Deimos finally zeroed in on his target. Throwing his head back, Deimos uttered a bizarre croaking bark. It took a second for Kael to realize that Deimos was actually laughing.

"You? You're the last one left?" Deimos roared, his voice thick with bloodlust.

"Are you scared?" Kael taunted with bravado. He wasn't ready to give up without a fight.

"Shaking in my boots," replied Deimos, lifting one foot out of the water.

Kael clenched his teeth – Deimos' "boots" were actually the skulls of dead competitors. At that moment, he realized exactly how slim his chance at winning this fight was. Kael was never trained in the art of combat. Sure, he was stronger and faster than most Humans by virtue of his race, but Deimos was not just any other human.

"She's not here to help you, is she?" Deimos baited, glancing up at the map in the sky.

Kael glared at Deimos.

"I knew she was still alive. You know she used you, right? She knew she couldn't survive on her own, not with me hunting her. Did you really think she would help you fight me in the end? Betray her own kind? You pathetic fool."

Kael lifted his pike and took a fighting stance. Deimos' upper lip curled and he bum rushed Kael, crashing through the beachhead barriers as if they were no more than toothpicks.

A howl erupted from Deimos as he stepped directly into a concealed trench filled with short sharpened stakes. He wrenched his foot from the trap and Kael could see that a stake had penetrated through, even past the alien skull boot. With as fierce a battle cry as he could muster, Kael lunged at Deimos, pike first.

Deimos parried Kael's first thrust with a thick forearm, sending a jolt through to Kael's arm. He caught the next thrust under his armpit and snapped the pike like a twig. In one swift movement, Deimos reached behind his back, unsheathing a makeshift weapon. It was a terrifying hybrid of saw and machete, carved from some poor alien's femur and fused with sharp teeth and talons. Although there was blood pooling into the sand beneath his foot, Deimos stepped forward menacingly in perfect balance.

Kael retreated into the tree line. There were other traps he could use to his advantage there and Deimos would have a harder time maneuvering through the trees. Or so he thought. Kael tried to lead the human through trap after trap, but to no avail. Deimos was apparently not going to make the same mistake twice. Nor were the trees impeding Deimos' approach – he simply hacked through whatever obstacle was in his way.

There was no choice left. Deimos was getting dangerously close and Kael would lead him right to Acara on the other side of the island if he didn't turn around and face him head on. And there was no way he was going to put Acara in danger, not after almost losing her once.

With a deep breath, Kael pulled the dagger from its harness on his leg. He held it in front of him, sideways and at the ready. He knew the weapon was no match for Deimos' but it was all he had left.

Deimos swung at Kael but Kael was too quick. The bone machete hacked the tree trunk Kael had been standing in front of clean through. With a roar, Deimos swung again. Another miss. Leaves were raining down upon the two fighters, obscuring their views.

Kael circled Deimos and darted in, slicing at the back of the human's knee. Deimos swung around in time to catch Kael squarely across the jaw with the edge of his plate shield. He went flying, landing in a rumpled heap amongst the fallen trees. Ears ringing, Kael struggled to his feet only to have Deimos to slice him across the chest with his bone sword. If not for the supply pack protecting his chest, Kael would have been eviscerated. Even with it, the wind was knocked from Kael's breast and he doubled over in pain.

He looked up just in time to see Deimos smile sadistically as he stood over him. He ripped off Kael's makeshift chest plate and tossed it aside, serving Kael a punch in the gut for good measure. Kael saw an opportunity and lunged forward with his dagger, lodging it in Deimos' thigh. He was rewarded with a backhand to the face that sent him sprawling once more, stars dancing in front of his eyes.

Deimos tossed aside his bone sword and plate shield with a maniacal grin and ripped the dagger free of his flesh as though it were no more than splinter.

"I'm going to enjoy killing you with your own weapon," Deimos growled.

He grabbed a fistful of Kael's hair and pulled him to his feet, slamming Kael against a tree so hard that he almost lost consciousness.

Kael heard rather than felt the sickening crunch of broken ribs as Deimos rammed him once again against the wood.

Pinned to the trunk by Deimos' thickly corded forearm, Kael realized in his semi-consciousness that he was about to die. He tried to open his eyes only to realize that they were already open and all he could see were shadows.

*I always though dying would hurt,* Kael mused. Strangely enough, he felt like he was floating.

A searing pain suddenly brought him back to full consciousness and he screamed, unable to contain his agony. Through the corner of his eye, he could dimly make out the hilt of his own dagger, plunged through his shoulder and into the tree, holding him up like some perverse scarecrow.

Deimos was grinning at him, cracking his knuckles in anticipation.

"You're the last one, you know. I gotta make it count. Something for people to remember," Deimos snarled. He yanked a tooth off his bone necklace, a cruel looking incisor that was at least six inches long. He held it up to Kael's eye, point first, preparing to ram it through his socket.

Kael slammed his eyes shut, flinching as he felt Deimos' hot breath in his face. He recoiled as a mist of hot liquid sprayed across his face. At first he thought it might be spittle, but the iron odor gave it away as blood. Kael opened his eyes to a sight that didn't make any sense.

Deimos stood in front of him, eyes staring down at his own chest. The tip of his bone sword protruded from his solar plexus, a silvery static discharge crackling around it. For a moment, nothing seemed to happen. Then, Deimos' lips parted as though to speak, but all that came out was a mouthful of dark red blood. It poured from his open mouth and trickled down his tightly wound muscles. Staggering, Deimos clutched at the air in front of him as though searching for something to hang onto. He finally keeled over, hitting the ground with a heavy thump. Kael couldn't tear his eyes away from Deimos as his body twitched in death.

"Kael!" cried Acara. She stepped over Deimos' body, his blood splattered across her cheek and running down her arms. With a firm grip, she wrenched the dagger from Kael's shoulder, freeing him. Kael collapsed to his knees, unable to stand.

Struggling under Kael's weight, Acara half-carried, half-dragged Kael to the water's edge. She eased him carefully into the waves so that his body was submerged to the neck but his head rested in her lap.

"I'm so sorry, Kael. I shouldn't have left you. I shouldn't have ..." Acara apologized, teardrops falling upon Kael's cheeks.

Kael could taste the salt of her tears mingling with the salt spray of the ocean and it was better than any balm he could imagine. He tried to reach up to touch her soft lips but he found that he couldn't move his right arm. Trying again with his other arm, he was able to bring it halfway out of the water before it, too, dropped.

"I'm not going to let you die, Kael," Acara whispered. She looked to the heavens, where only two red stars remained shining brightly in the sky.

"Do you hear me? I won't kill him!" Acara shouted.

"Don't do this, Acara," he tried to say, but all that came out was a ragged sigh.

He held on to Acara's visage as long as he could, admiring how the rising moons formed a glowing halo around her head even as his vision started to cloud. Then, all was black.

## Chapter Thirty
### Acara

Acara returned to the Human mothership, unsure of what her reception would be. She had been locked for days in negotiations on the Intergalactic Council mothership. After what had transpired in the Ring, no one was really sure how to proceed. Some people wanted to court martial her for murdering her own kind. Others wanted to hail her as an exemplar of the human species. All Acara knew was that she didn't feel like a traitor or a hero. She just felt lost.

"Don't worry – public opinion polls show that almost two-thirds of the human population sympathizes with the choice you made," Acara's cheery handler informed her as she was guided through the landing bay. "I, personally, would have done the same thing. That Eirlon was rather dreamy."

Acara winced. She didn't want to think about Kael. It was still too painful.

Familiar faces greeted her, mostly proud, some sullen, as Acara made her way to the main atrium. In her first public appearance since the Ring, Acara was more nervous than she had ever been before. The podium behind which she was to make her official statement to her entire species loomed larger than life in front of her.

Stepping up in front of the press pit, Acara scanned the room, feeling the gaze of hundreds of expectant eyes upon her. She felt exposed, even behind the microphones and pedestal. The President of Earth took the stage behind her, as did the Commandant, in a show of solidarity. The thought was of little comfort to Acara, especially given the private interactions she had had with President Roland on the Council Mothership.

The room became hushed in anticipation as the spotlight focused on Acara. On either side of her, screens lit up with images of her in her Champion gown the night before she left for the Ring.

*Was that really me?* Acara wondered.

The girl in the photo had long, flowing hair and a flawless complexion, with only the slightest hint of sadness in her eyes. She wore a robe bursting with color and fit for royalty. The girl standing on the podium wore a black jumpsuit adorned only with her rank. She had angry scars interrupting her right eyebrow and upper lip, as well as a freshly buzzed haircut. Her eyes held an edge that wasn't there before.

"Fellow humans, I am standing before you today in the hopes that you will understand the decisions I have made for humanity as a result of my actions in the Ring," Acara began, spitting out the canned speech she was told to recite.

Suddenly, Acara's gaze landed on the handsome man sitting in the back row, studying her intently. It was Axton. It had only been a month since she last saw him, but he looked like a new man. His hair was freshly cut so that it was finally in regulations. Acara could tell by his sharp civilian suit that he had been promoted to Councilor, and it showed in his bearing. Her heart swelled at the sight of him, and she realized what she needed to do. Axton deserved more than a rehearsed explanation, as did the rest of humanity.

"I know some of you think I am a traitor for killing another human. You might blame me for giving our victory away, and you might have every right to. But all of you watched me in the Ring. The bond I forged with ... the Eirlon is the same one that you forge every day with fellow humans – your family, your friends, your loved ones. And I could have no more allowed him to die than you could have allowed your loved ones to die.

But that's not what's important. What's important is that we now have a planet to call home. And it's a big planet, big enough to share with the Eirlons. We have a chance to rebuild, not just the Earth that we once knew, but a new, better home with new friends and new possibilities. Tomorrow, humanity descends on its new planet which will be called Plenus. The name is Latin for "complete," which it will be with both Humans and Eirlons working together to create a new world. The future is ours to mold, so let us forge a path together into the unknown."

The room was silent for a heartbeat and Acara held her breath. Then, the clapping began, lightly at first, but building quickly into thunderous applause. The cheers crescendoed as Acara received a standing ovation and for the first time since leaving the Ring, the weight on her shoulders lifted just a tiny bit.

Acara's handler spirited her away from the crowd. As she left the main atrium, Acara struggled to find Axton's face once more. It was impossible to see through the throngs of people now that she was no longer elevated on a dais.

"I need to talk to someone," Acara said urgently to her handler, who seemed to pay no attention.

"Sorry, dear, no time – you're expected on the Eirlon party ship in ten minutes," the handler tutted.

"No, really," insisted Acara, grabbing her handler's wrist. She clamped down a little harder. Now that she was wearing her biotic amplifier again, the energy amassed in her hand without her even needing to consciously summon it.

"All right, yes, not a problem, whom do you need to talk to?" the handler backtracked hastily, her eyes widening at the silver aura emanating from Acara's grip.

"Axton Fontaine."

"I need clearance for Axton Fontaine to enter docking station 422. Please notify him that his presence is required immediately at docking station 422," the handler chirped aloud through her communication implant.

Acara released her vicelike grip and her handler rubbed her forearm.

"Thank you."

## Chapter Thirty One
### Axton

She stood at the end of the docking station, arms crossed, gazing out of the view port towards the stars. Axton paused, his mind filled with thoughts of what he would say to her. The bullet wound had left a scar on Axton's body, but losing Acara had left a scar on his heart. He needed to set things right.

He reached out and touched Acara's shoulder tentatively, meeting her eyes in the reflection of the window. She turned around slowly, as though unsure of herself.

"Acara," Axton said huskily. Before he could stop himself, he enveloped her in a tight hug. He could feel her arms around his waist, squeezing him back. They stood, embracing, for what seemed like an eternity. Axton never wanted to let go again.

"Axton," whispered Acara, her voice breaking with emotion. She smiled up at him. "You finally got a haircut."

Axton gazed down upon Acara's upturned face and he had to fight an overwhelming urge to kiss her.

"So did you," he said, running his thumb lightly across her buzzed temple.

Moments passed as they stared at one another, looking for the familiar in each other and finding it despite how much they had both changed.

"I'm sorry," they both said at the same time.

"No, let me," said Axton, taking Acara's hands in his. "I'm sorry ... I said those things before you left. I ... I was hurt. And I was scared ... of losing you. I was stupid and wrong and I am so grateful that I have the chance to say that to you now."

"Axton, you don't need to …" Acara started.

"I love you," Axton interrupted suddenly.

Acara's eyes widened, her expression unfathomable.

"I've always loved you. Through everything," Axton barreled on, afraid that if he paused, he would lose his courage. "When I saw you in the Ring over the holotube … everything just … pulled hard to port. I hated feeling helpless, unable to do anything to protect you. I hated that someone else was there to save you. Not that you really needed saving. I mean, I guess I don't really know who either of us is any more. The Ring changed both of us. But maybe when things settle down … I don't know."

"Axton, I can't be with you," said Acara gently, taking her hands out of his. She rested a palm against his chest the way she used to before the Ring.

The words, though spoken kindly, were crushing to Axton.

"Do you … love the Eirlon?" Axton asked haltingly. He knew the Eirlon's name – everyone did. But he hated saying it.

It was a while before Acara answered.

"I don't know, Axton. I … care for Kael. But, I care for you, too. I … wish I had a better answer for you. But, that's not the reason I can't be with you."

"Whatever it is, we can work it out on Plenus. Like you said, it's a new beginning," Axton pleaded.

"I'm not going."

"Not going where?"

"I'm not going to Plenus. I've been granted command of a Lightjumper … I'm staying with the Armada."

Axton was at a loss for words. After everything that Acara had sacrificed and accomplished, he couldn't believe that she was willing to walk away.

"You're running away?" Axton asked, suddenly angry.

"No, I just ... I'm not ready to stay."

Silence stretched on as neither one could think of what to say next.

"Well," Acara said, finally. "I should go."

She stood on her toes and wrapped her arms around Axton's neck, kissing him lightly on the cheek, dangerously close to the corner of his mouth.

"I'm sorry. I ... wish we had more time together. Goodbye, Axton."

### Chapter Thirty Two
### Acara

Acara walked faster and faster until she was almost running away from Axton. She knew that if she looked back, she would be lost. A deluge of conflicting emotion had swept across her the moment she embraced Axton. She felt so confused. Part of her longed to go to Plenus with him, to explore what had been lost to them when she entered the Ring. The other part of her thought of Kael and how she couldn't imagine Plenus without him.

It took only a few minutes to find the ship she was looking for. The Eirlon design was distinct among the other vessels in the hangar, boasting a smooth white pebble-like shape in contrast with the hard angles of the human ships surrounding it. It was time for her final meeting with the Eirlons, the one in which she would tell them of her decision to stay with the Armada.

If anything, the Eirlon response to her had been overwhelmingly positive – much more so than the Human response. They treated her like a queen, with each crew member she passed on her way to the board room saluting her crisply in the Eirlon fashion.

By the time she arrived, most of the Eirlon dignitaries were already seated around a large circular table. The Earth President and Commandant were also present and given places of honor in the center of the table. The entire room rose as she entered, making her blush inadvertently.

"Please, everyone sit. I won't make you stay long – I have come to let you know that I do not plan to go to Plenus with the rest of my people."

A confounded chatter arose from the Eirlon side.

"But where will you go?" one dignitary asked.

"Who will rally Humans and Eirlons together?" another inquired.

"How will we transition in peace if you are not there?" pressed another.

President Roland called for order.

"Commander Price has been granted command of a Lightjumper of the Earth fleet. She will remain with the Armada as a Human representative of the Intergalactic Council. As she helped humanity find a home, she will do the same for other species throughout the galaxy," the President announced matter-of-factly. Even though he appeared supportive, Acara could still hear the bitterness in his words.

"I appreciate the support you've given me," said Acara. "I have no doubt that your people and mine will be able to build a new world harmoniously on Plenus, especially given the leadership of the people gathered in this room today. Not to mention Kael, whom you know is on the road to recovery and will be able to lend his wisdom and strength to your endeavors soon. You don't need me."

"But you shall be sorely missed," a wizened old Eirlon spoke up. Others nodded in agreement.

Acara bowed her head graciously, accepting the compliment. After a round of handshakes and goodbyes, she soon found herself wandering the corridors of the Eirlon ship. She knew where she would end up – outside a familiar door in the hospital ward, one that she visited every day since she was brought back from the Ring.

Cracking open the door, she was surprised to see that Kael was sitting up in his bed, propped by pillows. A wave of relief washed over Acara.

"You're awake!" she exclaimed, making her presence known.

"I awoke from my coma last night," Kael smiled. He held up a holographic tablet filled with Eirlon writing. "I've been catching up on everything that I missed. I see you somehow brokered an arrangement to save my life and share Eirlos, I mean, Plenus, between Humans and Eirlons. I'm grateful. And frankly, amazed."

"That's not exactly what happened behind closed doors," answered Acara truthfully. "But in the end, I've been saddled with all the credit ... and the blame. But it was worth it. I'm so sorry, Kael. You were my partner. I should never have abandoned you when you needed me most."

"I understand," said Kael. "What you had to do ... wasn't easy."

Acara smiled. She ran her fingers gently over the bandages covering Kael's chest and shoulder.

"How are you feeling?"

"Sore. But alive. Thanks to you."

"I ... I'm so glad you're going to be ok. I would never have forgiven myself if ..." Acara trailed off, unable to finish her thought.

"Come here," said Kael, making room for Acara on his bed. She nestled up next to him, feeling the warmth of his body through the sheets. She lay there for what seemed like a long time, unable to bring herself to let go of the intimate moment.

"You're not coming with us tomorrow, are you," Kael whispered into Acara's hair. It wasn't a question.

"No," Acara answered, not surprised that Kael knew of her plans. News traveled fast where a Ring champion was concerned. "It's different for you, Kael. You have something to go back to. I spent my entire life training to go into the Ring. And now that it's over, I realize ... I never really thought of what would come next. Not to mention that there is a vocal minority of people who think I betrayed the entire human race – it's a lot to live with. All I know is that I'm not ready to settle down on Plenus yet. I need time."

"And what about ... us?" asked Kael plaintively, propping himself up to face Acara. His violet eyes were dark with passion and meeting them made Acara flush.

"I ... I'm not ready for us yet, either," Acara replied. She knew it wasn't the answer Kael wanted, but she had to be honest. The past few weeks had been confusing and she was still reeling from the shock of everything that had happened. With Axton's words still ringing in her mind, Acara felt even more confounded by the emotions she was experiencing.

Kael sighed, but said nothing. Instead, he gently pressed Acara back so that she lay in the pillows. Acara's body tensed as Kael brought his body on top of hers, his lips just centimeters away from her own.

"I understand," Kael's voice was hoarse with feeling. "But if we have just this one night ..."

Acara realized then that she had been holding her breath and let it go with a shudder. Kael didn't have to finish his sentence – Acara could feel his intent. With every bit of pent up desire he had been withholding, Kael brought his mouth to Acara's, kissing her roughly with a mixture of lust and anger and love. Acara ran her hands over his smooth muscles as his lips grazed her neck. All her defenses finally dropped as she allowed herself to become lost in the moment, lost in Kael. If this was the only night they had together, every detail, every feeling would be seared into Acara's memory forever.

### *Epilogue*

Hundreds of Human and Eirlon ships disappeared into Plenus' atmosphere like burning rain drops hitting the ocean. Acara watched the magnificent sight from the bridge of her newly commissioned Lightjumper, the SSV Ulysses. A feeling of calm washed over her as the Earth mothership descended, the last of the Human ships.

Around the Ulysses, the other ships of the Armada began to jump out of the galaxy at faster than light speeds. Acara said a silent goodbye to Plenus as she ordered her crew to do the same.

"Prepare to jump."

"Yes, ma'am," the pilot answered over the comm link.

"Commander Price, coordinates locked," the navigator chimed in.

"Commander, light drives are online and ready to go on your command," announced a flight engineer.

Acara looked around at the crew – her crew. They had all volunteered for assignments on the Ulysses, placing their trust in Acara's leadership. Her pride swelled at the thought, the burden of responsibility a welcome weight on her shoulders, and she knew she had made the right choice. Maybe the void in her heart from giving up Axton and Kael would never be filled, but at least she had a purpose once more – one that was all her own. Being Ring Champion was a lonely fate, one that Acara would need to get used to.

"Commander, Lieutenant Fontaine reporting for duty," said a voice behind her.

Acara's heart skipped a beat and she spun around in disbelief. She ran through a full gamut of raw emotion in the space of milliseconds – surprise, anger, joy.

"Axton," she breathed.

There he was, standing in front of her, arm raised in a sharp salute, his bicep straining against his tight, rolled up sleeve. His new battle dress uniform suited him, tailored exactly to his form, the gray of the fabric bringing out the gray in his eyes. A dog tag chain peeked out from beneath his collar and shiny Lieutenant bars decorated his shoulders. With his new short cropped hair and freshly shaved face, he looked every inch a consummate soldier.

"What are you doing here?" Acara demanded, more with wonder than irritation.

"Heard the Ulysses needed a Weapons Officer, ma'am," replied Axton, lowering his salute. Though his expression was deadpan, his eyes twinkled with mischief.

"But ... what about Plenus? What about being a Councilor? Building a home?" Acara asked, unable to keep the bewilderment out of her tone.

Axton took a step closer to her, his eyes locked on hers.

"All this time, I thought that 'home' was a place. You made me see ... that 'home' is a person," he explained softly.

Moved, tears sprang unbidden to Acara's eyes. Her words caught in her throat as she struggled to comprehend the magnitude of all that Axton had given up for her.

"I ... I'm glad to have you aboard," said Acara, trying desperately to retain her bearing. Her heart pounded in her chest as she fought the urge to throw her arms around Axton.

A loud buzzer sounded, indicating that the ship was gearing up to jump. Axton stepped back.

"I'll be seeing you ... Commander."

Acara watched Axton leave as suddenly as he appeared, her feeling of loneliness dissipating. With a flushed face, Acara turned to the viewport just in time for one more glimpse of Plenus before the Ulysses warped away in a blur of light.

*Home,* she thought. *I am home.*